Roshelle Ramone truly has a gift.

Suddenly, it was as though the showroom of the Supreme Royale had been swept away and she was again Rachel Rayford sitting at the piano in the dusty little white-frame church in Sandott, Oklahoma.

She closed her eyes and the verses rolled forth. But something strange was happening. For when she played in Uncle Jess's church, God had been very real and very near. She *did* walk with Him and talk with Him. He *did* let her know she was His own. No aching loneliness plagued her then.

For a fleeting moment, there was the faintest recollection of His reality. It had been submerged into the darkest corners of her suppressed memories. The very act of playing, the familiar touch of the keys beneath her fingertips allowed her to travel back. It had been so long ago...since before her daddy died. But the memory was only a brief taste, then it was gone.

As the last notes of the chorus faded, she sat paralyzed. When she opened her eyes she found they were damp, and the applause was ringing once again. She rose on shaky legs and went to take her bows. She could make out a few faces in the front row, past the blazing spotlights, and found that some were crying with her.

NORMA JEAN LUTZ began her professional writing career in 1977 when she enrolled in a writing correspondence course. Since then, she has had over 200 short stories and articles published in both secular and Christian publications. She is also the author of five published teen novels.

Books by Norma Jean Lutz

HEARTSONG PRESENTS

HP41—Fields of Sweet Content

Love's Silken Melody

Norma Jean Lutz

Heartsong Presents

Dedicated to Angela (Angie) Hall, a dear
friend who not only loves Jesus
but is full of Jesus' love.

Special thanks
to Dr. Sheila Fenton and Andy Gilliam,
Cloud Nine Productions, Tulsa, Oklahoma.

ISBN 1-55748-447-3

LOVE'S SILKEN MELODY

one

Spotlights refracted into countless glittering stars against the performer's spangled turquoise dress. Deftly she moved out of the wings onto center stage. Her flaxen hair was in its usual simple elegant style—sleek and straight with bangs and the slightest curl at the ends.

Benny Lee's band exploded into throbbings that touched her feet like a magic wand. The muted lights melted from mauves to lavenders. Nervousness, tension, and worry were swept away by force. Roshelle never knew it to fail. Music drew her from the dregs, picked her up, and propelled her into dimensions high and bright.

Benny Lee, sitting at the piano, grinned at her. His smile, peeking through the full frowzy brown beard, inoculated her with confidence. Her step quickened. Why had she not heard it before? Applause—wild and crazy! Applause on an entry? Different. But something she could definitely get used to. Each club on this tour had been better than the last.

She grasped the mike and cold, solid metal contacted her damp palm. Nothing, no one, could stop her now. This was where she belonged. This was where she fit.

Benny Lee worked over the ivories, his bearlike form swaying slightly as he presented her with the smooth intro. Slowly, she raised the mike to her lips and the silken contralto poured forth a rich love ballad. Her slender body turned and moved with rhythmic understated motions.

When the music flowed, all else seemed to follow naturally. The melody spun out, a golden cord weaving listeners
into a captive trance.

Hadn't Benny Lee told her? "Stick with me," he said.
"We'll hit the tops together." He said it only three months
ago at that grungy little club in St. Louis where some klutz
was so obnoxious she actually cried over the incident. She
didn't want Benny Lee to see how upset she was for fear
he'd tear the guy apart. But the appearance of an occasional loudmouth wasn't the only problem. It was the whole
scene of second-rate places in which they'd played for
years.

When? she asked herself over and over. When would
the rooms be cleaner? When would there be an audience
who listened? Listened and perhaps even appreciated?

Then it happened. "This is it!" Benny Lee whooped
when he got the call from their new agent. At last a tour
was booked in something more than smoke-filled dives.
"Gen-u-wine uptown," Benny said. "Where folks wipe
their feet at the door. And," he added, "they kick out the
jerks without my help."

ROSHELLE RAMONE AND THE BENNY LEE CAMP BAND—the
words were surrounded by flashing pink lights on the
marquee out front of the sprawling Miami Beach Hotel.
Roshelle had seen it from her hotel window that afternoon
as she was working out her nervousness, dancing to an
aerobics tape.

If only she could take photos of the marquee and send
them to the folks back home in Sandott, Oklahoma. But
who would really care? No one back there had ever
understood her drive to make it to the top. Besides, how
would it look? Hardly the decorum of a famous enter-

tainer, to stand out on the street and take snapshots of her own marquee.

When the last full notes of the ballad unwound and came to rest, sweet applause came again to tickle her senses. Not a polite ripple, but real applause. "They're listening now," she wanted to cry out to Benny. "They're really hearing me."

Abruptly, the band moved uptempo. Benny began to bounce a little and Roshelle leaped into the rhythm like a racehorse at the starting gate—energetic, yet wisely paced. She moved to the golden stairs and descended to her audience, to sing to them personally—and they loved it.

Off the platform now, she executed a few complicated dance routines that caused another wave of rousing applause. At first she hadn't been sure, but now there was a heightened awareness of her control over them. A heady, intoxicating sensation. Benny Lee stopped playing the piano and raised his trumpet to his lips. The horn was now singing along with her in that teasing style of his. The guys in the band were sensing it as well. They were at peak performance, at the beck and call of their talented leader.

Never did Roshelle want another thing in life but to hold an audience spellbound as she was doing this moment. The exhilaration was unmatched in any other realm.

Effortlessly, she soared through several more numbers before taking a break. If only her body could keep pace with her heart's desire. Backstage, she stood for a moment catching her breath and noticed that Benny Lee was talking with the manager. From her vantage point it looked to be an agreeable conversation. Benny Lee was smiling. Then she stepped into the room where the boys in the band were unwinding.

Keel Stratton bent his thin torso into a deep bow as she stepped in the door. "Madam," he said, rising, then bowing again. "Oh, esteemed madam, to what do we owe this visit? That such an exalted celebrity should walk into the presence of these petty commoners?" Off came his coat that he twirled high over his head then spread on the floor. "Let not your dainty slippered feet touch the floor, your highness, but step only upon my humble cloak."

"Oh, Keel," she groaned. "Don't tease. I'm still in a million knots." She snatched up his coat and pretended to brush it off then threw it at him. He sidestepped, and it whizzed past him to the bar where Pedro Pedago was pouring a drink.

Pedro's dark eyes flashed as he mopped up the spill. "Hey, look out, Stratton. Maybe you don't care about stains on your jacket, but I do."

"Don't get your latin blood in a boil, Pedro. Besides, the lady threw it. Awkwardly, perhaps, but she did throw it."

Pedro tossed the jacket back to Keel who tossed it on the couch where Thorny Thorndyke and Mike Wilson were already engaged in a poker game spread out on the glass coffee table. Mike had pulled his glasses from his pocket and placed them on his nose. His youthful, studious appearance would have been more at home in a college dorm rather than being one-half of a quick poker game in the backroom of a nightclub.

"They're heartless," Pedro said to Roshelle as she looked over at them. "Ignore them. Their brains are pickled. Ginger ale?"

Roshelle nodded and took the icy glass from his hand. Why did reality have to be such a comedown? And yet she loved them all.

Mitzi Wilson, Mike's nineteen-year-old sister rushed in breathless and wide-eyed. "I've never heard you sing like that, Rosh. You were tremendous!"

"You always say that, Mitzi."

"Yeah, but this time I really mean it. Some big recording producer will hear you and you'll be swept away into stardom before our very eyes."

When Mitzi first joined their traveling entourage a year and a half ago, Roshelle was concerned that it wouldn't work out. Mitzi had run away from home—rather from a boring small community college as she put it—and found them in New Orleans. But, when Benny Lee learned she was a whiz at bookkeeping, he insisted she earn her keep. To Roshelle, the company of another female proved invaluable.

"You really were terrific," Pedro told her.

Before she could answer him, Benny came bursting through the door. He threw his burly arms around Roshelle and gave her a squeeze that lifted her off her feet. One glittery shoe flew off as he whirled her around. "They loved you, Rosh. They're crazy about you. You really wowed them. Just like I knew you would."

"Benny, put me down," she squealed. "I can't wow anybody if I'm seasick." She stood wobbly before him, but didn't move from his embrace. It was so safe to have Benny Lee holding her. He was like a fortress against all that posed a threat.

"I couldn't have done it without the band, Benny Lee, or without your help." She looked up at his puppy brown eyes. "Thanks," she whispered. "I can't believe we're really here."

Something grabbed at her foot and she looked down.

Keel bowed down to replace her shoe. "Hold still, your highness. Ah, at long last, one small favor this poor peasant boy can do for thee."

"Keel, let go of my foot or I'll wrap your drumsticks around your skinny neck," she warned, but she laughed as he placed her size five-and-a-half foot back into the slipper. "I'd better hurry if I'm going to get changed for the next number." Breaking away, she headed for the door. She turned back to look at them—her family. "Thanks again, guys. Mitzi, I'm wearing the emerald one next. Come help me zip up."

Minutes later the band was in place once again, playing her intro. By the time the show was closing down, Roshelle's body passed the exhaustion mark and moved into another gear fueled only by excess adrenalin.

"For my last number," her husky voice came over the mike, "I have a tradition that I've never broken in all my years of performing, and that is to close with a hymn."

Thorny and Mike put their guitars on the stands and Pedro laid aside his sax. Keel touched his brushes to the drums and cymbals as Benny Lee picked out the melody of *How Great Thou Art.*

The strains seemed out of place, but Roshelle wasn't one to go back on a promise. When Rosh was only sixteen, Grandma Riley had made her promise that no matter where she sang she would always close with a hymn. Many times she'd wished she'd never promised. But Grandma was gone now and how could she betray that precious old lady?

The applause that followed was a little weaker than previous ones. She gave her most professional smile and blew them kisses, replaced the mike, and disappeared through the curtains.

Still strung out in high gear, she headed for her private dressing room. Benny was beside her almost immediately. "Let me get you something," he said, closing the door.

"Ginger ale's adequate," she laughed, pressing her fingers to her temples.

"Rosh, I've told you a hundred times, you need something stronger at a time like this."

Her soft laugh sounded again. "Don't be so concerned, Benny Lee. I'm fine." She kicked off her shoes, and sunk into the couch.

Concern and unconcealed admiration for her shone is his soft brown eyes. "You're much more than fine, Rosh."

She knew by his expression that he wanted to say more, but she held up her hand and gave him a half smile. "The ginger ale, please. I'm plum dry."

When he returned with the chilled glass, in his hand was a tray on which was placed a nosegay of violets sprinkled with delicate baby's breath. They were lovely in their simplicity. "Benny! You old sweetie you."

"They're not from me, Rosh. You must've knocked somebody's socks off out there." He lowered the tray to her. "There's a card."

She reached out to touch the deep purple violets.

"Hey, does class scare you, Rosh?" He jiggled the tray. "Go on, take it. It won't burn. Probably some producer looking for a star just like you." He pulled the tray away abruptly. "Hey, what am I saying? I can't let someone bundle you off like that."

"Benny Lee!"

"Oh, all right. But you gotta promise to cut me in on a share of the take."

She laughed and shook her head. "You're impossible." Delicately she took the violets and sniffed their fragrance. There was a business card with them. "Victor Moran," it read. "President, Moran Recording Company." The address was Tulsa. She turned it over. In a bold script was penned, "Psalm 69:30, 'I will praise the name of God with a song. . . .' " Below that was written, "May I see you backstage?"

Roshelle stared at the card for a moment. A Bible verse—the last thing in the world she needed was a Bible verse. She gave a light laugh that sounded hollow even in her own ears. "What do you think?" She handed Benny Lee the card.

His expression sobered. "Sounds like a kook. I'll go get rid of him." He turned toward the door.

Roshelle straightened. "No, Benny Lee." She tucked a strand of blond hair behind her ear. "No. Let him come back. You can get rid of him if I give you the high sign."

Benny Lee looked at her. He had loosened his tie and the top button of his shirt was undone. To Roshelle, he always looked like a lovable teddy bear, and she did love him, but not in the way he wanted. She was wise enough to know the difference. Still, there was an unspoken knowing that Benny Lee had wanted their relationship to be more but Roshelle was determined that it remain on a friendship level. Now, he searched her face. "You sure?" he asked.

"I'm sure."

"Want to change first?"

"No, this is fine."

A moment after he left, there was a soft knock at her door. She rose to answer. There stood a tall man, slender, but not thin. His chestnut brown hair was softly styled back from his face. His impeccable gold-green suit, highlighting his gentle hazel eyes, was hardly what Roshelle had expected. The guy was a knockout!

"Miss Ramone? I'm Victor Moran. Thanks for seeing me."

Roshelle looked past him to where Benny Lee stood in the hallway, leaning against a doorway. "No problem," she answered, letting him in and waving him toward the couch. "Have a seat."

"Thanks."

"Sure." She stole a glance at him as he sat down. He looked nothing like a Bible-verse type of guy. The suit was obviously custom-made. He had an almost regal look, like a crown prince—narrow face, straight nose, hair perfectly groomed. A lot she knew about crown princes, she thought as she curled up in a chair across the small room.

"Tell me, Mr. Moran," she said coolly, "what can I do for you?"

"Please, just Vic. First of all, I wanted to tell you what an outstanding entertainer you are. I enjoyed the show tremendously." He leaned forward as he spoke. "I appreciate good music. Your voice has an almost silken quality. Quite unique."

Roshelle shook her hair back from her face. "You know what they say about an entertainer's ego. You certainly know how to feed it. Where did you derive your technique?" Did she detect a slight blush? How long had it been since she'd seen a guy blush? Eighth grade?

"I know it sounds a little plastic, but I'm as sincere as I can be. Your power and thrust are amazing. I also wanted to thank you for closing with a hymn. It takes courage to do that here, and I admire your fortitude. It's refreshing to see. The Lord will honor you for it."

Roshelle felt herself stiffen, as she remembered the verse on the card. "I appreciate the compliments, Victor—Vic but let's get one thing straight from the beginning. I sing those hymns for one reason and one reason only, It was a request of a dying granny to whom I couldn't say no. I've wished a thousand times that I'd never promised, but I did. I'm not and never will be Miss Goody Twoshoes."

"Still and yet, it does take courage—"

"Oh, sure. Courage to hear the volume of applause go down five decibels whenever I turn on the religious stuff? More insanity than courage, Mr. Moran! Sometimes, it quiets the drunks and makes the old men teary eyed. I'm far from being a saint and don't even pretend to be. But then, I'm not a hypocrite, either." Why was her heart pounding? Benny Lee was right outside the door and if she merely called his name, he would be dragging this guy out by his ear.

"Please, Roshelle. May I call you Roshelle?"

"That's my name."

"I had no intention of coming back here to upset you." His voice was quiet, even. His eyes were gentle. "On the contrary, I simply wanted to let you know what a blessing you were to me."

"Blessing? You even talk churchy. What's your bag, mister? What is it you really want? Invite me to a local revival?" Maybe he was one of those television ministers she'd heard about. Next, he'd be asking her to do a benefit concert to help raise money for his new multimillion-dollar television outreach. But still, she didn't call for Benny Lee.

Victor rose to his feet. "Scout's honor, Roshelle. No ulterior motives. I meant what I said. I simply wanted the violets to express to you how I felt about your performance. Beautiful flowers for a beautiful performance and a beautiful person. I'll go now, and I apologize if I upset you."

He pulled another card from the pocket of the silk suit and handed it to her. She didn't take it. He gently laid it on the glass coffee table. "Incidentally, you don't need to feel any certain way about a hymn for it to minister. The lyrics are based on Scripture. They minister life no matter how you feel about them." He gave her a quiet smile. "If you're ever in Tulsa, look me up."

"Oklahoma? Fat chance! It's a great place to be from— far away from."

"You're from Oklahoma?"

"Born and raised. No way you can make any money singing like I sing in Oklahoma. They don't like my style."

"On the contrary, I've heard some mighty spirited music in Tulsa."

"Tulsa, maybe; Sandott, hardly. Around my family— never."

He dismissed the negative comments as though she hadn't spoken them. "Thanks for letting me come backstage, Roshelle. I pray for the Lord to bless all that you do."

"Bless? Yeah. Yeah, sure. Thanks." When she closed the door and leaned upon it, she was trembling from head to stockinged toe. He had not called her a beautiful woman—but a beautiful *person*.

two

Roshelle paced the length of her hotel room, her night-gown swishing with each step, the carpeting plush beneath her bare feet. The applause had not ceased to thunder in her ears. The frightful exhilaration had wound her to a fever pitch and sleep had fled. The heavy draperies were drawn against the brightness of the lighted hotel front.

She snapped on the light in the bathroom and rummaged in her makeup case until she found the small prescription bottle. She didn't open it yet, but dropped it into the pocket of her nightgown and moved back out into the room. Sleeping pills were a last resort; she loathed the strung out feeling that came the next morning. She shunned the booze for the same reason. Her body was her friend and she was determined to take care of it.

Mitzi was asleep in the adjoining room. In the days of playing sleazy little dives on the back streets, she and Mitzi roomed together and talked and laughed all night.

"Now, Rosh," Benny Lee had said proudly, "on this tour, you get a room of your own. Class, angel. Lots of class."

But private rooms were intimidating to Roshelle, the solitude threatening. She didn't have to face it in a noisy bus, day after day nor in a crowded motel room with the giggling Mitzi. But now. . . .

She studied the door that led to Mitzi's room, then turned away. Cupping her elbows in her hands, she paced once more. A breeze had come up. She could hear it sweeping past her windows. Reaching for the fringed cords, she drew open the draperies. Palm trees swayed lazily and far out from the hotel grounds lay the ocean gleaming like a treasure in the moonlight.

Suddenly, she wanted to walk along that beach and feel the breeze in her hair. Fresh air. . .that's what she needed. She took off her nightgown and let it slip to the floor, hearing the bottle of sleeping pills make a soft thunk as it dropped. She changed into her royal blue sweats and a pair of sneakers.

Hopefully, Benny Lee, in the opposite adjoining room, would not hear her. She slid open the chain latch, wincing as it clanked. The door was heavy and groaned in protest as she pulled it open. The hall was dim and vacant. Just as she started to pull the door closed, she remembered. The room key! Tripping back in she grabbed it off the dresser and then closed the noisy door behind her.

Now, she could only hope there would be no drunks in the lobby to stop her and offer slobbery comments about the show. First, through the vast resplendent lobby and then to her left, down the hall to the open courtyard. So far, so good. Her sneakers were silent as she crossed the courtyard that also served as an outdoor snack bar; chairs were stacked on the tables now. Finally, the white beach lay before her. The breeze touched her hair and ruffled her bangs; she lifted her face to it. It was sweeter than she had imagined. She didn't slow her steps until she was at the foamy edge of the curling waves.

She stood with her feet planted apart and her hands on her hips looking out at the endless swelling and ebbing waves. In all her years of traveling with the band, seldom had they ever been on the coast. When they were, they were never on a nice stretch of beach like this.

Several times since she received Victor Moran in her dressing room, his quiet hazel eyes appeared in her mind's eye. Now, as she gazed out across the water, she saw them again.

Benny Lee's eyes were gentle and kind, always looking at her with tenderness and admiration, but they were also troubled eyes.

Victor Moran's eyes were not only gentle, but peaceful. They seemed to emit an essence of quiet. . . .

She shook her head to free herself of the clinging thoughts. Surely the breeze would clear away the sticky cobwebs. She turned to walk quickly along the water's edge.

She walked a ways in the silence, then "Rosh!" The voice coming down across the beach toward her made her gasp. She whirled around. It was only Keel.

"Keel, my word! You scared me silly. What're you doing out here at three in the morning?"

Keel slowed his long legs as he fell in beside her. "I might ask our fair celebrity the same question. What would Benny Lee say if he knew you were out here? It's not all that safe you know."

She gave him a guilty grin. "I know. He'd kill me, wouldn't he? But I couldn't sleep, and the beach looked so inviting from my room. Fresh air won over the pills tonight, Keel. At least so far."

"Great news. But the fresh air didn't win over Benny Lee. I think he's a trifle soused."

"So that's why he didn't hear me sneaking out."

"That's it." There was a moment of silence before Keel

asked, "Who was the flashy dude who gave you the posies tonight?"

Roshelle stopped and looked up at him. "Violets."

"Violets. Posies. Same difference."

"How'd you find out about it?" she asked with a trace of irritation.

"It was all Benny Lee talked about after he'd downed a few."

"Really?"

"You sound surprised."

"I guess I am. The guy was some sort of staid religious kook who wanted to make something saintly of my singing a hymn as a closer. That's all there was to it. No big deal. I've already forgotten about him."

Keel gently took her arm. "Let's sit down." He steered her away from the water's edge and sat beside her on the sand. "Did you explain it to Benny Lee?"

She dug her hand down into the sand and felt the fine grains sift through her fingers, and remembered. Remembered how she'd spoken to Benny Lee through the door after Victor had left. "I'm going to change and then rest a while," she'd told him. She hadn't admitted it before, but she didn't want to see him just then. More honestly, she hadn't wanted him to see her in her unexplainable trembling state.

"No, Keel, I guess I didn't explain. Should I have?"

Keel's voice was steady. The guy who was eternally kidding, was now too solemn. "You act like you don't realize what you mean to Benny Lee, Rosh."

"Keel!" She didn't want to hear this. Why should this skinny drummer try to meddle in her life? She started to get up, but he laid his hand on her arm. He didn't grab her, but his voice pleaded. "Just listen, Rosh. For a minute. Please?"

She nodded mutely and relaxed.

"Benny Lee could have handled it if you'd only explained everything. But when you wouldn't see him after the dude left, wild things began to play in his mind. He was even waiting and hoping he could throw the guy out. Those slick kind are a threat to him, Rosh. He's so scared of losing you. Why don't you just—"

"Marry him? Is that what you think I should do, Keel?"

"Why not? You're together constantly anyway."

"Did he send you to talk to me?"

"No! Like I told you, he's potted."

"So why did you decide to play cupid?"

Keel gave his silly laugh. "Honest, I didn't. You decided for me when you just happened to be out on the beach when I was coming out after the bar closed."

Roshelle mulled over what Keel had said. "Marriage is a trap, Keel. Why ruin a good relationship by getting bogged down in a rat race of marriage. Why spoil everything? If you think Benny Lee gets upset over guys like Moran now, what would he do if I were his wife?"

Keel shrugged his thin shoulders and she continued. "You have to understand—I'm headed for the top. Marriage has never fit into my plans. The ball and chain bit isn't compatible with a soaring career. I don't want to turn fifty someday and look back on four or five sour marriages polluting my career. I don't need that kind of misery. I'm chicken. I don't like pain. You may not think so, Keel, but Benny Lee understands."

"Do you talk about it?"

She paused. "No. It's just an understanding we have."

"It's an understanding you have, maybe. I don't think Ben understands at all. Maybe you should talk about it."

But that was just the problem, she protested inwardly. She'd never been able to talk about it to Benny Lee because of the way he looked at her. It broke her heart. What if she weakened? What if she couldn't stand strong?

Abruptly, she stood to her feet, brushing the sand from the seat of her sweats. "I think I'll sleep like a baby now, Keel. I'm going back to my room."

"Okay, I can take a hint. I touched a sensitive spot. But do us one little favor?"

"Name it."

"When you agree to see a flashy dude in your room, and then refuse to see Benny Lee afterward, at least give old Ben an explanation. It's a nightmare to get that lunk into the elevator and then into bed."

She laughed, thinking of the boys struggling to get their leader, built like a linebacker, into bed. "It's a deal." They were through the courtyard now and entering the lobby. "And Keel, thanks. I know it wasn't easy to say what you did."

"Psychoanalysis free! What a bargain." He laughed aloud in the empty lobby. She shushed him as the desk clerk looked their way.

"Mike says we're pulling out at ten in the morning," he said in a quieter tone as he put her on the elevator. "Be ready."

Roshelle was awakened out of a heavy sleep by sharp raps on her door. Who could be wanting her in the middle of the night?

"Go away," she muttered through the covers.

"Rosh, get up. It's me, Mitzi. Let me in so we can get you packed."

Turning over, Roshelle strained to focus on the clock. Nine o'clock? She felt as though she'd just fallen asleep. And Mike wanted to be on the road in an hour!

Shaking off the drowsiness, she roused and pulled on her robe and moved to let Mitzi in. On the dresser lay the violets. How awful! She hadn't even bothered to put them in water. How unfeeling she was. Just because she didn't like the giver was no reason to waste such beauty.

Purple violets and baby's breath. Representing innocence? What a joke. Mr. Moran had gotten the wrong idea about her. Courage for singing a hymn? What a laugh. If there was one thing she wasn't, it was courageous.

Still, Victor Moran was quite a mystery. Talking churchy, but looking nothing like the part. Strange. He talked almost like Grandma Riley, or Uncle Jess. . . .

No, she scolded herself mentally, you're thinking Rachel Rayford thoughts again. You buried Rachel to become Roshelle, remember?

"Rosh, good grief! Open this door or Mike will have a fit because we're late." Mitzi rattled the knob. "He'll blame me. You know how big brothers are."

"Coming, Mitzi. Keep your shirt on."

She'd heard of people pressing flowers, but what could she press them in? Quickly she tucked the little bouquet between the pages of a Bible she found in the drawer and slipped it into her suitcase, threw some clothes over it, and hurried to open the door. On her way past the front desk, she paid for the Bible.

When they got out front to the bus, Thorny and Keel were loading instrument cases and the drums into the storage bin of the bus. Keel grinned over at her as she and Mitzi approached.

"Our bags are ready and waiting in the lobby," Roshelle announced proudly.

"Terrific." Keel heaved in another case and shoved to adjust it into place. "Mike, go get the girls' things in the lobby."

Mike was sitting in the driver's seat scanning a map. "Get them yourself. I've gotta get this route figured out before we pull out of here."

"Where's Benny Lee?" Roshelle wanted to know.

Thorny jerked his head toward the hotel. "Coffee shop, downing the java. He'll be okay. . .sooner or later."

Roshelle stifled a groan. It was her fault.

"And Pedro's at his usual station," Mitzi added brightly.

Roshelle followed Mitzi's pointing finger to where Pedro sat with a woman on the edge of a fountain in front of the grand hotel. He seemed to be gallantly telling her how he hated to leave. Then he made a great to-do about saying goodbye. If she only knew, Roshelle thought. At nearly every stop, the handsome, dark-skinned sax player had a woman at his side.

Actually, Pedro's name was Ralph. But after Benny Lee hired him on and the boys heard his name, they laughed themselves silly over Ralph and promptly changed his name to Pedro!

Just then Benny Lee joined them, looking a bit tired, but hardy as ever.

She gave him her kindest smile. "Good morning, Papa Bear. Have you had your porridge?"

"Food! Perish the thought." He screwed up his bearded face and Mitzi giggled.

Thorny came pushing a loaded luggage cart. "Where's your trumpet case, Benny Lee?"

The hefty band leader came to life. "It was with the other equipment last night. Rosh, have you seen it?"

She shook her head. "Mike," she called, "where's the golden trumpet?"

Mike stuck his head out the bus door, the map still in hand. "I have enough trouble keeping track of my own stuff!" He retreated and a mad search was made throughout the empty club and then through the now-vacant rooms they had occupied. No trumpet.

"Rosh," Benny Lee said, "you know how I love that stupid old thing. We've just gotta find it." They were walking back to the bus.

"I know, Ben. I know. Don't worry. We'll find it."

"You don't think it could have been stolen do you?"

"Who'd want a battered old trumpet?"

He laughed. "This is true."

"Time to get loaded and head on down the pike," Mike warned as they approached the bus. Pedro was hurrying toward them from the fountain area and in his hand was the missing trumpet case.

"Pedro," Rosh yelled at him. "What are you doing with Benny Lee's trumpet?"

Pedro looked down at the case as though he'd just discovered it and then grinned at them. "I was guarding it. Anyone who would leave their trumpet in the men's room of a bar ought to hire a keeper."

Benny Lee threw back his head and let his deep laughter roll. "Am I a dunce or what? In the men's room! Boy, I must be getting old."

"If that's everything, then let's get rolling!" Mike

ordered in the gruffest tone his young voice could muster.

"Give a man some authority," Thorny muttered as he boarded, "and it all goes to his head."

Mitzi shook her head. "Organized confusion as usual," she said with a giggle.

Within minutes they were loaded, settled, and on their way in the spacious bus.

"Hey, Rosh," Keel called out from the back where he was already raiding the small propane refrigerator. "Hear any more from your religious freak of last night?"

He was doing it for Benny Lee, Roshelle knew. "Why no, Keel. I guess I sent him packing when he found out what a heathen sinner I was."

"Yeah, well," he called back, his mouth full of a ham sandwich. "Good thing you set him straight."

"Religious freak?" Benny Lee looked at her.

"That guy who sent the violets and the Bible verse."

"Oh yeah, I remember."

"He was just a kook like you said. I should have let you throw him out in the first place."

"Wish you had." He slid down in the seat to take a nap.

The next night the little group landed in Mobile for a week's stand. After that, New Orleans. The tour then took them north to Little Rock, St. Louis, and on to Chicago.

In St. Louis, there was a small greeting card waiting for her from Victor Moran. The card was lavender with a dusky photo of violets on the front. The note read: "You've been in my thoughts and in my prayers." Benny Lee didn't see it. She hid it in her suitcase.

It was March and they had left spring behind in New Orleans where the flowers were blooming. It was snowing in Chicago.

"That crazy agent doesn't even know how to schedule a tour," Roshelle complained to Benny Lee in her dressing room after the first show. "That white stuff out there is definitely a bummer."

"Newt's the best agent we've ever had, Roshelle. If he's crazy, he's only crazy about the way you sing!" He poured her a ginger ale. "Better not complain. This is the best money we've ever earned. Besides it's the windy city, remember?"

Another lavender card awaited her in Chicago. She wanted to be angry. The nerve of that guy! And how did he know her itinerary? The note read: "Wish I could see how Chicago receives a hymn. Bless you, Vic." She threw it across the room. Later, she tucked it into her suitcase with the other one.

Two days later, she had just returned to her hotel room from a strenuous workout, jogging the marvelous indoor track. The phone was ringing as she came in the door. Still out of breath, she answered. It was Newt, calling from Los Angeles.

"I've been meaning to talk to you," she teased. "Is it sunny there? Well, it's freezing out here. We slipped and slid all the way up here in that old bus."

"Okay, Rosh! You don't like the chill? How does Reno sound? I don't think it's snowing in Reno today."

"Reno? That's a long way from Chicago, Newt. You got us a spot in Reno?" In her mind's eye she could see him rolling an unlit cigar between his fingers as he talked.

"Tentatively, you're booked in Reno. From there, with a little loose finagling, looks like I could get you into Vegas. This guy's got a club in Vegas and if he likes you—"

"Vegas?" She had gone from breathless to totally winded. Unceremoniously, she collapsed back onto the bed. "You mean it, Newt? I thought it would be years before Vegas."

"It's not one of them flashy joints on the strip," his nasal voice sounded back at her. "But it's not bad for starters. What do you say?"

"Let me talk to the boys. I'll call you back in an hour."

"Hey, Rosh. Hang on. Tell me. Did you hear me say anything about a band?"

Painfully, Roshelle sat up and stared at the phone in her hand. No words came. Her brain refused to compute. "No, Newt," she answered in a weak whisper.

"Now listen, sweets. Bands aren't too big right now. A dime a dozen. Get it? But you? You got class...style... a powerful voice. I can sell you, easy. Look, I been working on this thing night and day for a week. What do you say? Are we on?"

"The boys and I have been together forever."

"Hey! Look who's getting sentimental. The last time you were in L.A., you told me you wanted to go to the top. Am I right, or was I dreaming on a sauerkraut sandwich?"

"You're right, Newt. That's where I'm heading."

"So what's a few musicians along the way. They was doing fine before you met them. Dump them and get on with the business at hand."

Dump them? It sounded so harsh...cruel...heartless. She needed them and they needed her. "I'll have to talk to them before I can say yes. Surely you understand that."

"So talk. But make it quick. This guy in Reno just had a cancellation and he's sort of up a creek. I need you out here, pronto. Oh, and by the way, I've been talking with a recording company to boot. They like your sound."

Roshelle ran her fingers through her soft bangs. They settled, featherlike, back onto her forehead. "I'll call you back right away."

"See to it, sweets. I'm in a hurry to make both of us rich."

"Oh, Newt?"

"Yeah?"

"Thanks."

three

Had Roshelle been flying alone, she would have pulled down the shade on the plane window. The takeoff from O'Hare in the driving snow was terrifying, adding anguish to her already frazzled nerves. But perky Mitzi insisted on having the window seat and, like a little kid, kept peering out. After all, it was her first flight!

Above the snowstorm, cloud formations spread out like pink marshmallow fluff. Roshelle turned her red-rimmed eyes from the brilliance. Why did things have to turn out this way? she questioned silently. Wasn't this the break she'd waited for since she left home and played her first club in Tulsa?

So why had she let herself get so attached to the band? Like Newt said, they were just a bunch of musicians. But they'd become so much a part of her.

Benny Lee had held her close to his massive chest after she explained everything to him. "Maybe it'll only last a few weeks," she told him. "Even if I go on to Vegas, I'll be with you again after that."

"Rosh," Benny Lee said in his gentlest tone. "Don't you cry, Rosh. You're gonna make it, angel. You're gonna make it big. Just like you always dreamed. And when you do," he dabbed at her tears with his handkerchief, "you call for us and we'll be there in a flash. We'll be coming up to where you are, not you falling back down to where we are."

29

But the words didn't make the hurt go away and when she left them at the airport, she felt like Dorothy saying goodbye to her friends in the Land of Oz before going home to Kansas. Keel was definitely the Scarecrow. Mike, the Tinman. She'd edit in two crazy new characters for Thorny and Pedro because Benny Lee, of course, was her lovable Cowardly Lion—only with courage unlimited.

But, unlike Dorothy, she wasn't going home. She didn't have a home, really. But it never mattered. With a mobile family, who needed a home?

It was Mike's idea for Mitzi to go with Roshelle. He wanted better things for his baby sister. But, for whatever reason, Roshelle was thankful and Mitzi warmed up to the idea immediately.

"Put her to work," Mike had said. "She knows the ropes. She can be your personal secretary."

It sounded good, personal secretary. Plain old down-home company sounded better.

"Hey," Benny Lee protested to Mike. "What do you think you're doing, giving away my bookkeeper?"

"I guess I'm brilliant enough to keep your simple books," Mike shot back at him.

But they were just going on, as they always did. How she would miss it. The zaniness of it all, the rushing, the hurrying. Mike ordering people around like he owned them. Keel's wit and wisdom. Pedro and his women. Thorny and his poker. And Benny Lee. . . .

Roshelle snuggled the luxurious blue fox jacket around her face, more for comfort than for warmth. It was her very first fur. Benny Lee insisted on getting it for her before she left. "You'll have a jillion furs soon enough, Rosh. All I ask is to give you your first one."

"You look great in the fur, Rosh," Mitzi piped up next to her, as though she had a readout on Roshelle's brain waves. Her wide, brown-black eyes were dancing. She reached over and stroked the sleeve. "Feels so. . .so money!"

"It gives me an almost wicked feeling to wear it."

"Wicked? Why? You look terrific."

"Blue fox," Roshelle mused. "Sounds like something at the top of the endangered species list."

"Female vocalists are on the list, too, Rosh. Just figure it was them or you."

"Thanks."

"Oh, don't worry, honey. Mama Mitzi is here to take care of you."

Roshelle looked at her youthful companion who reminded her of her younger sister, Janey, who was always giggling and joking, too. Mitzi's black, close-cropped curls framed a pixie face. She looked nearer to fifteen than almost nineteen. Roshelle was six years her senior. "Okay, Mama Mitzi," Roshelle mocked, laughing at the irony of it. "Take over."

"I'll be in the wings, tomorrow night, Ms. Ramone," Mitzi sing-songed, "and I'll have your endangered species jacket ready for you to wear out on your third curtain call. Won't that be flashy?"

"Third? Hey, I like you. You think big!"

"You're that good, Rosh. They'll love you!"

"Forget the wings, Mama Mitzi. I'm planting you in the audience to lead the applause." That led them both into enough giggles to attract stares.

Later, Mitzi asked, "Rosh, are you going to play your

own accompaniment like Benny Lee suggested?"

Roshelle thought a moment, running her fingers over the hem of the fleecy jacket. "I guess I can answer that better when I've rehearsed with the combo there. See how we mesh."

"You play a mean piano. Just take over and do your own thing."

"It isn't that, Mitzi. The problem is lack of audience contact when I'm at the keyboard. It stands as a barrier between me and my audience. I love to move among them. The music is ministering to them and I want them to know that I know it."

Mitzi turned to look square at her. "Ministering? That's a funny word coming from you. I've never heard you say that before."

Roshelle hedged. "I don't mean minister exactly."

What was it that Victor had said? That the hymns minister life. Had he planted the word in her brain?

"I guess I mean help," she corrected herself. "Uplift. You know. I give them something they can reach out and take hold of. And what do you mean, funny word? Don't forget, I was raised in church."

"I remember. Your uncle was a minister, wasn't he?"

"Of sorts."

"That's an odd answer. Was he, or wasn't he?"

"He had all the right papers, but all the wrong actions."

"One of those who doesn't practice what he preaches? There are a lot of his kind around."

"My Grandma Riley preached a better sermon than Uncle Jess, and she never stepped foot in the pulpit."

"Did you ever play the piano in church?" Mitzi wanted to know.

"Almost from the time I could reach the keys." She remembered how proud Daddy had been the first time his little Rachel played for the congregational singing on a Sunday night. For a time, she was only allowed to play on Sunday and Wednesday nights, when the crowds were smaller. But when the regular pianist suffered so badly from arthritis that she could no longer play, Uncle Jess let Roshelle play on Sunday mornings as well. She could play every song in the song book, and some that weren't.

"Did you play all those years? Until you ran away from home?"

"Actually, no. When I got a little older I stopped. Sort of in rebellion, I guess."

When Daddy died, she swore she would never do anything for Uncle Jess ever again. Uncle Jess called it "wicked rebellion" that was "bound up in her heart." But she didn't care what he said. She sat staunchly on the back pew of the church and refused to play for him. It made her mother furious.

It was her fault the conversation had veered in this direction and now she wanted out. The memories were as painful as ever. Fortunately, at that moment, the pilot announced their approach to the Cannon International Airport. Thankfully, Mitzi let the subject drop.

"I suppose there'll be a big black limo to pick you up," Mitzi remarked as she stuffed the flight magazine back into the pocket of the seat in front of her and fastened her seat belt. "What a kick."

But there was no limo. Nobody. . .nothing.

"Now, where did I put my women's lib handbook," Mitzi quipped as she grabbed for their luggage and pulled them off the moving carousel. "How did I ever become so dependent upon men?"

"You should have memorized the handbook so you could teach me. What's a good secretary for anyway?"

By the time all of their luggage had been retrieved, a porter had spotted them and offered his assistance. And, with his kind assistance, they were led to the car rental office and were soon loading the luggage into the trunk of a nice little compact car.

"This is more my speed than a limo, anyway," Roshelle said after tipping the porter and coming around to the rider's side.

"Hey," Mitzi called out. "Where're you going?"

Roshelle stood on the curb and looked at her. "You do drive, don't you, secretary?"

Mitzi raised innocent eyebrows. "Drive, I do. Have my license, I don't."

"Some personal secretary!" Roshelle fumed. "Well, get in and we'll try to find the Supreme Royale Hotel. Shouldn't be too hard. Help me look." As they craned and watched, Roshelle muttered, "First on our list will be for you to take your driver's test and get your license."

Mitzi shrugged, unaffected. "How was I to know I was up for promotion to a chauffeur? Somehow a license never seemed important. I never liked doing things that were legal."

Roshelle shot her a sidelong glance.

"Until now, that is," she added with a giggle.

The Supreme Royale was a new hotel in Reno. Tall and glittering in the sunshine. Not nearly as spectacular as some of the others, but not bad considering where she'd come from, Roshelle thought.

She was scheduled to appear in the cabaret rather than the bigger theater showroom. Obviously, that was why she had to sing with the existing musicians. Rehearsals with the combo were frightful. During a break, she sat down in the front, away from the stage, and pondered her predicament. It was a good combo. . .uptempo. . .versatile. Not as versatile as Benny, but good enough. Perhaps it was simply the adjustment time. How naive she'd been, leaning so much into Benny Lee's music and style. She should have been developing on her own style. . .in her own way. Well, better late than never. Silently, she determined to work hard to adjust and to be her own person and have the band follow her direction and lead.

The stage was the most elaborate setup Roshelle had ever seen—massive shimmering sets in bright luminous colors. She tried not to appear awestruck as she sat there studying it.

The band leader, a short serious man named Truman, came bouncing down the stairs toward her. "Everything to your liking I trust, Ms. Ramone?" he asked politely.

"Thank you, Truman. A little more latin emphasis on the second number, please. And tone down the drums when I go into the bluesy number near the break."

He nodded and pulled a small notebook from his pocket and took down neat little notes. She would learn to work with others. She really would.

"By the way, I sing a hymn at the close of all my concerts."

Truman cleared his throat and looked at her. "A what?"

"A hymn. A church song, you know, like. . .like 'Rock of Ages.' "

His expression was as unchanging as that rock. As

though to say, "One more screwball, more or less, makes no difference." What he did say was, "You want the band to play a hymn?"

She felt herself weakening. "The band doesn't have to play. Why don't you just have the pianist follow along."

He nodded, his face still a mask. "Anything else, Ms. Ramone?"

There were other things...several other things. But this was all she could handle at the moment. She shook her head and said, "No."

He rose to leave.

"Thank you, Truman," she called after him, feeling that her last contact with success had been severed.

That evening, she followed a mediocre juggling act that was no buildup for her at all. The band came through tolerably, though not as superbly as Benny Lee's band would have done. There was rousing applause, which was heartening.

The next afternoon, she was able to boldly talk to Truman about the other things that needed altering. He was still amicable, but somewhat distant. If ever she would have given up on the hymns, this would have been the moment. Obviously, the pianist didn't like the idea of playing a hymn and his delight was either to drag it or rush ahead. She simply had to make do.

On the second evening, following the show, Mitzi was rapping on the dressing room door. Roshelle invited her in.

"You have company, Rosh. A group traveling together." She was flushed and giggling. "You'll never believe this."

"Must be the Local Morticians Association."

"Almost. A group of senior citizens. A whole flock of gray-haired women."

Roshelle gave a dry laugh. "What a following. What a way to crack Reno." She let out a deep sigh. "Invite them back, I suppose. But don't leave me. And when I give you the high sign, shoo the hens out. Got it?"

"Got it, boss."

There were only about a dozen of them, all cackling and fussing over her just like a bunch of mother hens. They seemed terribly excited about her dressing room. One in particular reminded her of Grandma Riley. "Bless you, child, for singing the hymn right in the midst of the heathens."

Roshelle wanted to ask her what she was doing in the midst of the heathens, but she refrained.

After Mitzi had "shooed" them out, Roshelle didn't know whether to laugh or cry. . .to feel privileged or humiliated.

What she did feel was a fresh acute wave of loneliness that she couldn't free herself from or even define. That night she took sleeping pills. There was no beach.

Toward the end of the second week, Newt called to confirm she was booked at the Supreme Royale in Vegas. "Same song, second verse," he quipped. "It's not Caesar's Palace, but it is Vegas. The guy says you did good there in Reno and he thinks you could make it in Vegas as well. He says the audiences like your 'traditional' style. What a break, sweets. We're going places. I'm still working on the recording deal. I'll keep you informed as it progresses." Newt always did most of the talking. Patiently, she listened as his nasal voice talked around a chewed cigar.

All the while she strove to keep her heart still. Vegas! She could almost taste it.

"Oh, and Rosh, this fellow won't squawk if you have your own accompanist. I pressed him about it for you. Rosh? You still there? I said—"

"Yes, I heard you, Newt, my own accompanist. Accompanist, not band?"

"Yep."

"So where's Benny Lee so I can call and tell him?" Her heart was hammering hard now. If she could just have Benny Lee with her in Vegas, then everything would be all right again.

She motioned for Mitzi to get her a pen as Newt rattled off the number of a place in Jersey City. She then waved Mitzi out of the room as she punched phone buttons with unsteady fingers. Let him be there, her heart cried out.

In a hollow well, she heard the hotel clerk paging, "Benny Lee Camp! Phone call for Benny Lee Camp!" Eventually, his deep voice was on the other end of the line.

"Camp here!"

"Hi, Benny Lee."

"Rosh! Hey, Angel. What's the good word? Super to hear from you!"

"I'll be playing the Royale in Vegas in a few weeks. They like my style, they say."

"Terrific news, Rosh. I knew it. Didn't I tell you? Go for it. Give it all you got."

"Benny Lee, I just got the word from Newt—at the Royale in Vegas I can have my own accompanist." It was quiet for a moment. Now her heart was thudding in her brain. "My own accompanist, Benny Lee. Can you come out? We can work together again."

"Rosh," he said softly. "I can't, Rosh. You know I can't. The boys. Remember what we said? We'll all come when you need us. But I can't just leave them. They'll scatter like the wind. And we're in the middle of a tour, remember?"

Of course she knew all that. She knew from the beginning that he couldn't come. But he should come to her. Wasn't she more important than the band?

"But I need you, Ben. I need you here." She was being totally self-centered, like a spoiled child. If Benny Lee did not come, she would still have her pick of pianists. But if he came to her, the boys would have no leader. . .no band . . .nothing. It was as though she couldn't help herself. The loneliness. . . .

"This tour will be over in six weeks, Angel. I won't schedule another thing. I promise. We'll hang loose till we hear from you, okay?"

"Six weeks! The world could come to an end in six weeks. I need you now, to play for me in Vegas, Benny Lee. Are you coming or not?"

"Rosh! Please! Be reasonable. Don't ask me something you know I can't do."

"Oh forget it then!" Her voice was high pitched, ugly. "I don't need you or anybody! Forget I ever called!" She slammed the receiver down with a crash.

Now the sobs were coming hard. How could he care more about them than her? What a stinking rotten mess!

"Rosh," Mitzi was banging on the door between their adjoining rooms. "Rosh! Let me in."

"Hold on, will you? Let a person get herself back together."

She stumbled into the bathroom and splashed cold water

on her mascara-smeared eyes, then let Mitzi in.

"You should have known he'd say no."

"I don't pay you to listen in on my conversations," she snapped as she slouched into the plush chaise by the bed.

Mitzi was oblivious of the curt manner. "I didn't need to listen, silly. I knew what he'd say. After all, that's what we all love about Benny Lee—his staunch loyalty." She busied herself at the wet bar fixing Roshelle an icy lemonade.

Of course she was right, but Roshelle didn't want to hear it.

"Well, you were right about one thing," Mitzi said calmly.

"What's that?" She sipped on the lemonade, thankful for it's sharp tartness.

"You don't need Benny Lee. Not really. You can do it, Rosh. You can make it on your own. Now, get those gorgeous eyes repaired. Rehearsal's in ten minutes."

Mitzi was turning out to be one great secretary.

The next week, they caught an evening flight out of Reno. Now it was Roshelle's turn to stare out the window as they circled McCarran Airport. Las Vegas lay as a sparkling, glittering broach on the breast of the desert. She could almost feel the pulsating beat of its vital energy pumping up into the airwaves. Names like Golden Nugget, Horseshoe, Showboat, and the Sahara smiled and winked at her, beckoning her into a new world.

"Get ready," she whispered to the twinkling lights below. "Here I come."

The pair of them rubber-necked like tourists all the way from McCarran to The Strip. Roshelle had been in Vegas one time previously with Benny and the boys, before Mitzi had joined the troupe and so she tried to point out the sights to Mitzi. But even Roshelle was gawking, so much had changed. Neither the Excalibur nor the Mirage existed when she and the boys played a small club off The Strip those many years ago. The five-storied waterfall at the Mirage would make anyone stare. And whether or not they wanted to stop to watch the volcano erupt, they were forced to because the line of tourists ahead of them was stopping.

The Royale was at the north end of The Strip. A tall gleaming building with a flashing neon crown above the words SUPREME ROYALE. The causeway was lined with swaying palm trees and curved around and into little bridges spanning man-made lagoons. As they stepped inside from the golden porte-cochere, they entered a fantasy wonderland. A tri-level atrium was accented with bubbling marble fountains laced with lush tropical plants and trees. Massive crystal chandeliers hung suspended from the highest points of the ceiling.

"Bugsy would never recognize the place," Roshelle whispered, looking around.

"Bugsy? Who's Bugsy?" Mitzi whispered back. "We don't know anyone named Bugsy."

Roshelle looked at her friend and smiled. "Bugsy Siegel, silly. The guy who masterminded this city in the first place."

"Oh. Never heard of him."

As soon as the young man at the desk learned who they were, he called management. They were quickly shown to their suite on the tenth floor. The room they walked into was done in tones of autumn gold and forest greens. Soft brocade couches, teakwood furniture, sunken tub in the bathroom—they were both in awe.

When they were alone, Mitzi ran to the window to look out. Roshelle looked, too, but refrained from running.

"Rosh," she cried, pointing like a little kid, "the clown from Circus Circus is over there laughing at us."

"Laughing *with* us, not *at* us. He's happy we're here. And so am I."

Rehearsals the next afternoon went off without a hitch. The band leader was a swell guy, affable and jocular and easy to work with. But Roshelle wasn't going to get caught in a pinch this time. As they conferred privately, she quietly explained that she would need the piano pushed center stage for her last number. He agreed with a smile and a nod.

"Opening night jitters?" Mitzi quipped as they took a few laps in the hotel's indoor pool that afternoon.

"An over-extended, exaggerated, extreme case of jitters, if you please."

"Well, cool it. You'll do great."

"Keep telling me." She dove in to challenge Mitzi to another race down the length of the pool.

She won easily, jumping out at the shallow end and grabbing for her towel. Briskly, she wiped droplets from her eyes. As she took the towel from her face, she caught a glimpse of a man dressed in sweats walking through the weight room adjacent to the pool. Her breath caught. It looked exactly like Victor Moran.

She fluffed her hair with the towel and shook her head vigorously. Impossible. If there's one place a religious guy would never be, it was Vegas. There had been no word from him since Chicago. Hopefully he'd forgotten about her. She thought she'd forgotten about him, too. But perhaps she hadn't. Otherwise why would she be looking at total strangers and thinking it was him?

She was so keyed up by curtain time, she virtually exploded onto the stage and never wavered in thrust or energy throughout the entire performance. The warmup group was excellent, setting a mood of expectancy in the audience. Gracefully she moved from one number into the next, talking gently with her audience between each. Her sultry voice cast it spell over her listeners. She felt as though she could sing forever.

She slowed to a low-keyed ballad and the wailing of the trumpet cried along with her. They forced the music before them in an unhurried blazing crescendo that brought people to their feet.

Now the piano was center stage. Slowly, she moved toward it. It had been years since she'd played in a performance. But some things, she thought ruefully, you never lose.

In a momentary panic, she realized she hadn't planned which hymn to sing. But, as her fingers rambled up and down the keys, she effortlessly moved into the simple strains of "In the Garden." Her voice could do nothing but obey the promptings from deep within.

> "He walks with me, and He talks with me,
> And He tells me I am His own.
> And the joy we share as we tarry there,
> None other has ever known."

Suddenly, it was as though the showroom of the Su-

preme Royale had been swept away and she was again
Rachel Rayford sitting at the piano in the dusty little white-
frame church in Sandott, Oklahoma.

She closed her eyes and the verses rolled forth. But
something strange was happening. For when she played
in Uncle Jess's church, God had been very real and very
near. She *did* walk with Him and talk with Him. He *did*
let her know she was His own. No aching loneliness
plagued her then.

For a fleeting moment, there was the faintest recollection of His reality. It had been submerged into the darkest
corners of her suppressed memories. The very act of
playing, the familiar touch of the keys beneath her fingertips allowed her to travel back. It had been so long ago
. . .since before her daddy died. But the memory was only
a brief taste, then it was gone.

As the last notes of the chorus faded, she sat paralyzed.
When she opened her eyes she found they were damp, and
the applause was ringing once again. She rose on shaky
legs and went to take her bows. She could make out a few
faces in the front row, past the blazing spotlights, and
found that some were crying with her.

This was insane. People in Vegas cry only when they
lose at the game tables.

Then she saw him—Victor. There, off to the side. He
was smiling at her. So he *was* here. This was all his fault!
Somehow his being here had done this horrid thing and had
yanked her back into the morass of the past. She main-
tained her facade, smiling, taking bows, and blowing
kisses until she made it to the side stage where Mitzi
helped her to her dressing room.

"What were you saying about a piano being a barrier?"

Mitzi said. "You weren't at the piano, Rosh. You were sitting in their laps. They loved it!"

Mitzi opened the door and let Roshelle in ahead of her. There, on the counter, beneath the brightly lit makeup mirrors, was a tray with a nosegay of violets and a card.

four

Roshelle stood still a moment, staring.

"What's the matter?" Mitzi asked, closing the door. Then she saw, too. "Oh. It's that religious guy again, huh?" She moved past Roshelle to look down at the unpretentious little bouquet. "This is like the bouquet he sent to your room in Miami, isn't it? Violets?"

Roshelle only nodded. She wanted to run. She wanted to cry. She wanted to throw the silly flowers in the trash. What right did he have?

"They're sort of cute." Mitzi reached down for the card. "Shall we. . .?"

"Don't touch that!"

Mitzi drew back her hand as though she'd touched a hot iron. At the hurt look in her eyes, Roshelle was immediately sorry. "I didn't mean to snap at you, Mitzi. But this guy sort of gives me the creeps. I saw him in the audience out there tonight."

"He's right here in Vegas? The religious guy? Don't that beat all."

"Will you stop calling him 'religious?' "

"Well, isn't he? I thought he gave you a Bible verse and stuff. That's what Keel said."

"How about the word, 'Christian?' "

"Same difference. You called him a religious freak."

"Correction. *Keel* called him a religious freak." Roshelle recalled the conversation on the bus as though it were

46

yesterday. "I called him a kook," she added softly.

"The guy spooks you and you split hairs about what the nut should be called." Mitzi shook her head in confusion. "What's the deal here? Do we open the card or not?"

"*We* are not going to do anything. I think I just need to be alone for a few minutes, okay? I need to sit down until my head stops spinning."

"Hey, Rosh. Now it's my turn to apologize. Come and sit down here." She hurried to fluff pillows on the couch situated against the far wall. "Do you want to change now? Later? What can I get you? I'll put the flowers in water and then I'll get you a ginger ale."

"Please, Mitzi. I think I really do want to be alone for a few minutes."

"I didn't mean to make you mad," Mitzi said.

"I could never be mad at you." She reached out to give her little partner a hug and felt tears still near the surface. Mitzi gave a squeeze in return. "I'm glad. I think you're the greatest."

Surely it must just be the excitement of the first performance in Vegas. That's all it was. And yet Roshelle was sure that once the tears started, they'd never stop. That's how uptight she felt. And now this. She wanted to read that note, but she couldn't bare to do it in Mitzi's presence.

"Okay, boss. I'm going. But not far. Just holler if you need me. Got it?"

"Thanks."

Mitzi moved toward the door. She paused and nodded toward the flowers. "Don't let this little thing bug you. You got too much going for you." And she was gone.

How did this guy find so many lavender cards? She opened the lavender envelope and pulled out the card. A picture of violets covered the front. Inside he had written out his praise for her evening performance. At the bottom he added an invitation to lunch the next day. "Call me," it said, "Room 875." Psalm 69:30 was added again as well. Of course, she couldn't go. How she wished Benny Lee were here. She needed his presence to protect her from all the crazies in this world.

There was a soft tap on the door. "Psst. Roshelle. It's me, Mitzi."

Quickly, Roshelle slipped the card back into the envelope. "What is it?"

Mitzi opened the door and stuck her head in, her dark eyes flashing. "The 'Christian-religious-freak-nut-kook' is headed this way! Want me to guard the door?"

Vic? But the card asked her to call. Why would he come back to her room? She needed time to think.

"Quick, he's. . .well, hello, Mr. Moran. How are you tonight? And what brings you to Las Vegas?"

Roshelle could hear him asking if he could see "Miss Ramone."

"I'm not sure," Mitzi told him, hedging. "She's so exhausted after that long performance. Do you realize how much energy it takes to perform that many songs?"

"I won't be long," she heard Vic answer.

"Mitzi," Roshelle called out. "It's okay. I'll see Mr. Moran."

Mitzi stuck her head back inside the door with a questioning look. Roshelle nodded at her. "Just for a minute," she said.

Mitzi shrugged and withdrew. "She'll see you just for a minute, Mr. Moran. Please don't tire her."

Roshelle had to smile at Mitzi's new stance as her

guardian. And before she could take a breath, there he stood in the doorway, seemingly twice as handsome as the first time she saw him. Impeccably dressed in a hunter green suit that reflected warmth to his hazel eyes.

He smiled and closed the door. But not before Mitzi raised her voice to say, "I'll be right out here, Rosh."

"You're well taken care of," he said, nodding toward Mitzi.

"Mitzi's great," she retorted. She felt awkward, unsettled. What could he want?

"Did Mitzi replace the big bearded fellow who was with you in Miami?"

"Benny Lee? Oh, no." Then she paused. "Well, sort of, I guess." Mitzi couldn't take the place of her buddies in the band, but she certainly had filled a void.

"The booking didn't include the band?" It was a question and statement combined.

She shook her head, thinking again of the pain of having to leave them.

"Couldn't you have insisted? Held out?"

She looked at him. "You don't do much insisting in this business when you're first starting out. You should know that." But actually, she had no idea what this man did know about the business. Probably very little. "This night has been a big breakthrough for me." She hated being put on the defensive. "Benny Lee and the guys insisted I take the offer."

Vic nodded. "I see you got the violets."

Was he fishing for a response? She inwardly vowed not to give him the pleasure, so she only offered a slight nod. Moving to the mirrors, she poured herself a cup of coffee from the coffee maker on the counter. "Want a cup?"

"Thanks, I'll pass. I promised your little friend out there I'd wouldn't keep you. In the note I invited you to lunch tomorrow, but I was wondering if you'd rather make it a picnic out at the lake."

Roshelle emptied a packet of sugar into the mug of coffee and stirred it with the plastic stir rod. "Lake? What lake?"

"Lake Mead. You know, where Hoover Dam is. The area near the lake is filled with nice picnic spots. Less than an hour's drive away. There's more to this region than blazing marquees and roulette tables."

"I never was very good at geography." She sipped at the scalding coffee. Sitting beside a lake sounded glorious to her right now. Water was always so peaceful. Like the beach. Like the pond at Grandma Riley's that was surrounded by weeping willows.

"We could grab sandwiches at a deli and leave at about ten. I'll have you back in plenty of time to be ready for your afternoon rehearsals."

He knew enough to know she was in rehearsals late in the afternoon. But how would a Christian know...? "Are you here on vacation?" she asked, letting her curiosity win out.

"Business, actually. One of my clients has a show in town. I wanted to catch it."

"But your card said you had a *Christian* recording company." She wondered how he was going to explain his way out of this. Probably works with gospel quartet groups in Tulsa and several "swingers" out here in Vegas.

"I do. It is." His voice never wavered.

Her own voice was not so steady. "Then what. . .?"

"I understand your confusion. We—meaning my company—don't happen to think the Christian faith is to be imprisoned within the confines of a church building. Several of the stars who record on our label feel we are to 'go into all the world,' as Scripture says. And that includes Vegas."

That was absolutely the dumbest thing she'd ever heard. A Christian singing in a nightclub. In fact, she wasn't sure she even believed him. And why should she? She didn't even know him.

A tapping at the door let them know that Mitzi was getting restless. "Roshelle, can I get you anything?"

"Thanks, Mitzi. I have coffee. Everything's fine."

"Just checking," came the answer through the door.

Vic gave a low chuckle. "She's marvelous." He moved to go. "The picnic? What do you say? A little sunshine, fresh air, and quiet."

Surely he wouldn't be a threat to her. And the offer sounded tempting. "Okay, Mr. Moran, I'll accept that offer of the fresh air."

His smile was soft and subdued, not as though he'd won a victory, but of quiet acceptance. "Great. I'll meet you in the lobby at ten. And the name's Vic."

"Thanks, Vic. And thank you for the flowers."

"My pleasure. I've never seen or felt a more moving moment in a Vegas club as I did during your last number. There wasn't a dry eye in the place. You deserve all the accolades. Bless you now."

Bless me, bless me, she fumed inwardly. Always blessing me. Immediately she wanted to defend herself. But he opened the door, gave a little salute, and was gone.

Give a guy an inch and he'll take a mile every time. Well, she had his room number. She could always call him and cancel.

Mitzi was by her side in a flash. "Man, oh man, that's the best looking kook I've ever laid my eyes on. Wonder if he has a brother?"

Roshelle collapsed into a chair laughing. "You're hopeless."

"Come on, Rosh. Don't tell me you don't think he's a knockout." Mitzi rummaged in the small refrigerator for a soda, popped the top, and took a long drink. "If you don't, I'll take you in tomorrow and get your eyes checked."

Roshelle avoided a direct answer. "If you're so hep on him, forget about the brother. Vic is obviously not taken."

"Yeah, but he's not sending me darling little bouquets." She picked up the delicate nosegay from the table and arranged them in a cup with water. "There. That'll do till we get them up to your room." She fingered the lace around the flowers. "Wonder how he thinks of something so original? Most men don't have a clue. So what did he want?"

"If you must know, Miss Snoopy, he's taking me on a picnic tomorrow."

"Whoa. You mean you're actually going out with him?"

Roshelle hadn't thought of it like that. . .not like a date. She'd never dated, not really. Her high school years were so abnormal. Uncle Jess always spying on her. . .her mother's strict rules. Then later, there was Benny Lee. "It's not like I'm 'going out with him.' "

"No? So what do you call it?"

"We're just going to take a little lunch and go out to the lake."

Mitzi nodded, drank the last of her soda, and threw it into the waste basket. "Like I said, a picnic-lunch date."

Roshelle picked up a pillow from the couch and slung it toward Mitzi, but she ducked. Mitzi picked up the card from the table, put it under the cup holding the violets, then reached down to help Roshelle up from the chair. "Ta-ta now. Let's get you up to your room, so you'll be fresh for your picnic-lunch date tomorrow."

Roshelle groaned as she rose from the chair. "I think I'll ship you back to your brother."

By the time they arrived at the room, there was a massive bouquet of roses waiting them. "Congrats on cracking Vegas. From Benny and the boys," the card read. Roshelle felt the tears burning. She'd never known such an ache of emptiness before. When she left home, she never missed anyone. Not Janey, not her mother, and especially not Uncle Jess.

"Let's call them," Mitzi was saying, excitement bubbling in her voice.

Roshelle glanced at her watch. "Do you realize what time it is on the east coast? About four. They've crashed. And you know how hard it is to get Benny Lee awake." She couldn't bear the thought of actually talking to the guys. Not the way she felt right now. It would only make things worse.

"Oh, yeah." Mitzi looked deflated. "You're probably right. It'd be almost impossible to get any of them awake enough to talk."

Roshelle hadn't even thought of how much Mitzi must miss her brother. Mentally, she kicked herself. "Tell you what. Tomorrow you call Mike and tell him all about our success here tonight. In fact, feel free to call Mike anytime. Newt will always know where they are."

Mitzi's pixie face brightened. "Oh, Rosh. I'm so silly.

I didn't even think that it would be okay to call him anytime. I really do miss the nut."

"He's family, Mitzi. You should keep in close contact."

Mitzi moved toward the door that separated their rooms. "They're all family to me, Rosh."

As soon as the door was closed, Roshelle let the tears loose and they didn't stop until she had cried herself to sleep. The next morning, she still couldn't figure out why she had cried.

five

The drive to the lake was peaceful, as Vic had promised. They left the bustling city of Las Vegas and entered the rugged countryside. Farther down the highway was the quiet community of Boulder City. Past that lay the mammoth lake.

Roshelle had wanted to wear shorts but, knowing Vic's background, she opted for a comfortable skirt, blouse, and sandals. After all, hadn't Uncle Jess reminded her on countless occasions of the utter sinfulness of wearing shorts? "No decent girl would be caught dead in them," he declared.

When they met in the lobby, she was quite surprised to see Vic dressed in olive shorts with a white knit shirt open at the throat. She was tempted to run back to her room and change, but she let it go. Nothing about this guy made any sense.

"I have a large tablecloth," he said as they spotted the lake in the distance. "Shall we cover a picnic table with it, or spread it out and sit on the ground?"

"Oh the ground, most definitely. The tables are for the wimps."

He gave a little laugh. "I see."

She craned to see the appearance of the lake and in a few moments it was spread out before them. The indigo water was ringed by craggy mountains and bluffs ranging in color from sandy tan to blue-black. Wispy clouds hanging low in the sunlit sky seemed to be snagging on the tops of the bluffs as they sailed by them. Situated in the inlet was a large marina with rows of stanchioned sailboats sitting with their masts pointing skyward. In the distance, little sailboats scooted along like feathers across the water.

"Let's sit as near to the water as possible," she said.

"I'm sure that can be arranged."

And it was. He parked in a picnic area that was nearly deserted and pointed down the incline to a wide flat ledge that jutted out. "How does that look?"

"Great."

Vic handed Roshelle the tablecloth and he followed behind, carrying the cooler.

"Do you always come to Vegas packing a cooler and such a nice tablecloth?" she queried him.

"I confess. I have friends who live here in the city and I went borrowing early this morning."

As she spread the cloth, she felt the lake breeze softly ruffle her hair. She turned her face to it and closed her eyes and breathed in deeply. "M-m-m. Sometimes I forget how much I miss the openness and the fresh air. Clubs and hotels can be pretty stifling at times."

"You're a country girl, I take it?" He was digging in the cooler and pulling out sandwiches, fruit, and cooled bottles of soft drinks. The food looked wonderful. She'd had no breakfast.

"Not really country but definitely small town. Until I was a teenager, anyway."

He handed her a sandwich. "Do you like ham and cheese?"

"I'm not fussy."

Before she could unwrap the sandwich and dig in, Vic said, "Let's take a minute and thank the Lord for the food and for His handiwork at creating this beautiful spot."

She felt her teeth clench. She'd not said grace since she left home. It was always a big joke to hear Uncle Jess pray—no matter what the occasion.

Vic's prayer, however, was nothing like Uncle Jess's. Vic seemed to be talking to more than just the air. But, regardless, Roshelle was glad when he was finished and she could devour her sandwich.

"So," Vic said as he leaned back on one elbow, "when will you have your band back with you?"

She shrugged. She wasn't sure how much she wanted Vic to know about her or her business. "My agent seemed vague about it."

"Is your agent in L.A.?"

Her mouth was full, so she nodded.

"What's his name?"

"Newt."

"Hardcastle?"

"Yes. You know him?"

Vic offered her a bunch of grapes and she took them. "I've had dealings with him in the past. He's good. All business, that's for sure."

"That describes Newt." Roshelle recalled the night he instructed her to dump the band. She still wondered if she had made the right decision. "He sure put us on the map. He seems to have all the right connections."

"I know. That's why it surprises me that he couldn't book all of you together in Vegas."

"He said bands are a dime a dozen."

Vic nodded soberly. "Well, he does have a point there."

"Maybe when we begin recording sessions."

"Maybe what?"

"Maybe Benny can be with me again."

"Don't count on it."

"Why do you say that?" She wasn't sure if it was his words or the wind off the lake that made her shiver.

"Have you been in a recording studio lately?"

"No, not for a few years." Roshelle thought of the small little studio in Tulsa where she had spent hours recording ad jingles for everything from car dealerships to furniture stores. But that was nearly six years ago. Six years! Had she been on her own that long?

"Everything is done by computers now. Those keyboards can make a trumpet sound as good as your friend, Benny Lee. And of course the percussion sounds are superior to any drummer's."

Immediately in her mind's eye, Roshelle saw loose-jointed Keel banging his drums, ecstatic every minute of every performance. She shook her head. "Imagine that. Tough for the musicians."

"Of course, later on, if you're on a nationwide tour you'll need them. Or if you have a few big hits. Then you can record in one of the nicer studios with space enough for an entire orchestra if you want one."

That all sounded so far away. She hadn't thought about her time without Benny being so drawn out.

"How did you meet him?" Vic wanted to know. He was gathering up scraps of their trash and putting it in a bag in the cooler.

"Newt?"

"No, Benny."

She had to smile as she thought of it. How Benny practically rescued her from a bar owner in Little Rock. The creep wasn't going to pay her until she came through with a few favors. But Benny saw to it she was paid. And quickly, too. But how could she tell Vic about all that mess? So she simply said, "At a cheap dive in Little

Rock," and let it go at that. When she met Benny, she was doing okay. . .not great, but at least okay. She was getting more and more job offers and was traveling more. But joining with the band was a smart move. She helped them, and they helped her.

"When was that? How long have you worked together?"

She had to stop and figure it out. "Almost five years. Boy, it doesn't seem that long."

He studied her face a moment as though he meant to ask another question. She was relieved that he didn't. Instead, he stood to his feet. "Want to walk down by the water?"

She jumped up. "Sure."

They loaded the cooler back into the car and made their way down to the water's edge. "Let's wade," she said, pulling off her sandals. The shore was full of painful little rocks, but she didn't care. Vic kicked off his loafers and tucked the socks inside.

She couldn't help but laugh as she felt the cold waves lapping up against her legs.

"Your laugh is almost as silken as your singing voice," he said softly.

Roshelle felt herself blush. "Thanks."

"How did you learn to sing? To play the piano? Voice lessons? Piano lessons? Your performance last night was a knockout."

Last night was something she was trying to forget—at least the moment when those strange feelings emerged as she played and sang the hymn. Performing nightly for all these years had sharpened her ability to act. She'd leaned how to press the emotions down and put on her stage face. No matter how you feel at show time, a performer puts on the stage face and the stage smile. She did that now.

"I can't remember not singing," she answered lightly. "My mother says I was mimicking the radio when I was about three. They quickly learned to be very selective of what stations they listened to."

Vic chuckled at that remark.

"I even sang all the zany ads. But when I learned how to turn the dial myself, then I did have fun! I sang all the hits."

"Pure and natural God-given talent," he said with a touch of wonder in his tone. "And the piano?"

"My Grandma Riley. Mother's mother. She taught piano in her younger days. The trouble was, she taught me solely out of the hymnbook. With a few classics thrown in for good measure."

"What a blessing to have that kind of a background."

She gave a little snort. "I guess it's all in how you look at it. It was like prison to me. At school, I ransacked my music teacher's sheet music stash and played everything I could get my hands on."

He laughed. "That figures. But at least you had God's Word around you as you grew up."

"All I remember is being surrounded by a bunch of hypocrites—all except for Grandma—and I detest hypocrites."

He gazed out across the water, squinting his eyes. "You're in good company then."

"Meaning?"

"Jesus didn't take to them very kindly, either."

She looked up at him. She thought he was making fun of her, but his face was quiet and sober. The hazel eyes were not teasing. She looked down at her watch. "We'd better be getting back. I've still got a big day ahead of me." As she turned to go, she caught her foot on one of the rocks and started to fall. In a flash, Vic reached out to grab her arm and steady her. She fully expected him to take her in his arms—and for a split second she wanted him to. She stood there for a moment looking up at him. Soft hazel eyes looked steadily back at her. "Thanks," she whispered, then pulled free.

Later, she scolded herself for being so vulnerable. She would have to be on her guard constantly. No Benny here to keep watch out for her. When she arrived back at the hotel, she marveled that this Christian had not once preached to her or dictated his demands on her life. That in itself was a miracle.

Roshelle opened the door of her room to see Mitzi sitting on the bed, meticulously painting her toenails. She lifted the brush in one hand and the bottle in the other, as if in a salute. "Ah, she's back from her first date. And now tell Mama Mitzi all about it."

Roshelle pushed the door shut with her hip. "There's nothing to tell. We drove to the lake and had a picnic and came home."

Mitzi finished her little toe with a flourish and replaced the brush in the bottle. "The guy is so good looking, how did you keep from just melting away?"

"I kept an ice pack on my head," she commented dryly. She opened the closet to pull out slacks to wear to rehearsal.

Hobbling over, walking on her heels, Mitzi said, "Truly Roshelle. His eyes remind me of old Paul Newman movies. They're so. . .so bottomless. How can he be a kook and be so dreamy?"

Roshelle hated it when Mitzi spoke her very thoughts. "Would you help me find a blouse to match these slacks? I have to be at rehearsal."

"You have almost an hour and you have three blouses that match those slacks." She leaned against the wall beside the closet. "Do you kind of like him? Just a little bit?"

"He's okay." She pulled out the silk paisley with the huge puffy sleeves. "Does this one go?"

"Yeah, but you look better in the mauve."

"Which mauve?"

Mitzi reached around and rummaged through the blouses. "This one." She extended the blouse, then put it behind her. "And I'll give it to you when you tell me what he's really like."

Roshelle reached for the blouse but Mitzi stepped away. "If I knew, I'd tell you," she protested. "The guy's a closed book."

As soon as she said it, she realized what a dumb statement it was. She had asked him little or nothing about himself because she was scared to ask. But Mitzi was right about the eyes. Roshelle knew leering eyes. She knew condemning eyes. She knew troubled eyes. But never had she seen such peaceful eyes. And they were bottomless. Like you could get lost in them.

Mitzi was now across the room waving the blouse. "Does Mama Mitzi have to teach little Roshie how to *open* the book?"

"Mama Mitzi better give over the blouse if she doesn't want to eat it *and* have her fine little pedicure stepped on." She stomped in Mitzi's direction.

In a flurry of giggles, Mitzi sprinted for the bathroom. "Since you don't know how to even read a book, tell me one thing. If he asked you out again, would you go?"

Yes, yes, her mind cried out. But she stifled the words. Aloud she said, "I might."

The blouse came flying through the air—hanger and all. "That's all I wanted to know."

"Mitzi Wilson, you're impossible. Help me find my shoes."

With a brief goodbye, Vic left for Tulsa later that week. Roshelle breathed a sigh of relief. Now she could let down her defenses. Since opening night she had carefully avoided singing "In the Garden." Usually she stayed with something more rigid, like "A Mighty Fortress is Our God." But even then, Vic's presence in the room always gave her spooky sensations. She wondered why he continued to show up. Until the day he left town, he attended every show.

Night by night the size of her audiences grew. As Mitzi so aptly said, it was absolutely "titillating" to see the warm response. From L.A., Newt called with updates on the upcoming recording sessions. He, too, was delighted with the Vegas success.

"Hey, sweets," he said, "you know Ann-Margaret was discovered in Las Vegas. Don't happen very often, but methinks it's happening now."

They were down to talking about song selections for the CD when Newt suggested she rent a place in L.A. "You'll be here for a while, till we get this CD cut. No sense in you women hanging around in a dead hotel," he said.

It was a novel idea and one she'd not thought of before. After all, there was money now. More money than she'd ever seen while singing with Benny and the band. Why not rent a place and sort of set up housekeeping? The idea was strange and nice all at the same time. Later, she went to Mitzi's room to run the idea by her.

"You bet," she agreed. "A Malibu beach house would

be to my liking." Mitzi had been at the pool most of the afternoon and was fluffing her short black hair with a large gold hotel towel. She'd managed to gain a luxurious tan in the few weeks they'd been there. "With a pool, naturally."

Roshelle laughed. "I don't think we're quite to that point yet. But we could get a place and have a home base. That makes sense doesn't it? I mean even if we go on tour, which Newt says we probably will if the CD takes off, we'll still need a place." Mitzi turned to her, peeking out from under the towel. "Are you trying to convince me or you? I'm fine wherever you put me."

That was so true. Mitzi was like a little flower blooming through the cracks in a boulder. Roshelle never saw her get ruffled. She envied her friend's even disposition...her quietness. Roshelle's nerves seemed to be in a constant jangle and the only time she was truly calm and happy was during a performance.

"Newt says he can talk to a realtor friend for us and maybe find a condo or something. And there *could* be a pool, maybe even a yard."

"Cool." Mitzi was now in the bathroom and turned on the hair dryer thereby ending the conversation for a few moments.

Roshelle continued to see a little place that would be her own. She sighed and lay back on the bed. Maybe that was what she needed. A place to put down roots, instead of bouncing all over the country like a ping-pong ball. Maybe then she'd have more of a sense of peace.

Rolling over, she grabbed the phone to give Newt the go-ahead to begin the search.

Roshelle's last performance at the Supreme Royale was

both exhilarating and frightening. Frightening because she had no idea where her career would take her from this point. The questions tugged at her mind as she readied herself for the show.

As sort of a gift to celebrate the success of the run, Newt had secured a wardrobe stylist for her. Louis Sarviano was his name and he had created a stunning black, sequined gown as one of her outfits for the closing night. It was strapless with trails of black organza draping from the back to the floor.

When Mitzi first learned about Louis she giggled. "Want me to hang around in case he tries to tuck a dart in the wrong place?"

Roshelle laughed, too, but she did indeed want Mitzi to be there for every fitting. Louis had laughing blue eyes and dark hair that hung in curls down the back of his tan neck. His open smile revealed a set of wonderful dimples. Roshelle was ecstatic that Newt had sent him up to Vegas just for her. Louis was a professional, and he knew how to make her look good. But then, that was his business— making people look good on stage.

She turned around in front of the three-way mirror in awe of the image before her. She looked like a million, and felt the same.

As soon as her feet hit that stage, it was as though they were sprinkled with magic dust. She danced almost as much as she sang. The dress was more like her skin and it moved with her every move. Her husky voice was never more strong, never more powerful. Her confidence soared.

Traditionally, she opened with the jazzier numbers to set the tone. From there, she slid into the blues, where her voice melded with the trumpet in an aching ballad. The long wailing notes wove a web around her audience and fastened them to her. They forgot their cocktails and the clamorous casinos, as she spun out the sad words of the love ballads. She hung on to every note, not wanting them to end. . .not wanting this magical night to end.

Much too soon, the piano was being rolled to center stage for her finale. She tossed the hand mike to the closest engineer and sat down on the padded bench. Without a thought, her fingers traveled up and down the keyboard. And, unbidden, "In the Garden" came rolling forth. She wanted to stop it but it was too late. As before, she once again felt herself sitting as Rachel in the little church in Sandott. But rather than feeling a godly presence, there was Uncle Jess's eternal scowl denouncing her, condemning her. "You're nothing but a Jezebel," the words flew at her. "Your soul's bound for hell, girl. You'll never amount to anything!"

The emotional blow was so crushing, she could barely finish the song. The response, though, was not diminished, but she could barely hear the warm applause. Mitzi had to support Roshelle's weight as they headed to the dressing room after the third bow.

"Three curtain calls, Rosh. Just like I said." Her voice was edged with fear. "Let's get you in here and let you rest. A magnificent performance. Absolutely magnificent."

After Mitzi had settled her in the room, Roshelle looked up at her. "Can you get me something to use to gargle? My throat feels funny. Kind of scratchy."

six

She and Mitzi were both deliriously happy with the cozy little condo Newt found for them in Anaheim. With a pool! "Nothing highbrow," Newt had told them, "but comfy."

First on Roshelle's agenda was to purchase her own piano. The room they designated as her studio was painted in the palest banana yellow and furnished with inviting pastel seating pieces and white lacquered coffee tables. Splashes of California sunshine poured in through tall windows that were flanked by bookshelves—shelves that she planned to fill with wonderful books, in addition to all her music.

There in her "studio" with her new piano, she poured herself into her work until she knew every nuance of every song scheduled for the upcoming CD. She'd been practicing her numbers nonstop since she arrived in L.A. In spurts of new inspiration, she was even penning lyrics and melodies of her own.

When Newt presented her with the recording contract, she used it as an excuse to call Benny to ask his advice. She closed the door to the studio so Mitzi couldn't hear. Mitzi would want to talk to all five of the guys; Roshelle needed to talk to Benny alone.

He gave a whoop when he heard her voice. "I hear you knocked 'em dead in Vegas, Rosh! I knew you would." It was as though her last angry tirade with him had never happened. What a teddy bear he was. "Now you got a contract with the Laurel label. I mean, you're on your way."

When she asked him about the fine print and secret clauses, he simply told her to trust Newt. "He's the best in the business I ever saw, Angel. He'll do you good. You don't have to sweat that."

She wanted him to tell her to send him a copy to look at, or even to say he'd fly out and take a look. But he didn't.

"You'll have to fly out soon and see our little place, Benny. I have a home just like normal people. Mitzi and I are buying furniture and house plants and fixing it up spiffy."

"Hey now, ain't that right uptown. A place of your own? Careful or you'll get domesticated on us."

"Not hardly. So when can you come out?"

She could hear him mumbling something as he thumbed through the dogeared calendar he always carried. "Newt's got us sewed up for another six weeks or more. Not even breathing room. Sorry, Angel. Not soon, but then that don't mean never. We'll be heading out that way sooner or later. We always do."

He was right. But he sounded so vague.

"You still there, Angel? You're so quiet. Do you think I don't want to see you? If so, you're wrong. I miss you like crazy. But I just don't see how I can. . . ."

She took a deep breath and straightened herself. "It's okay, Benny. Really. Just come when you can. Okay?" She knew Benny. He kept everything buried.

"That's my girl. We sure will. We'll all be on your doorstep when you least expect it. Then you'll have to scramble eggs for the whole bunch."

For his sake, she managed a light laugh as they said their

goodbyes. She knew the separation was killing him, but he was holding it in. And she kept making it worse. And why? Why did she even think it would be better if he came? She pushed her fingers to her throbbing temples. Perhaps it was like being weaned from a security blanket. She'd leaned on him totally for almost five years.

She moved from the phone to the piano and began another strenuous session of work. That night she took several sleeping pills to get to sleep.

The Laurel recording studios were in the Valley, only a few miles from Newt's office. Roshelle could remember when a recording studio was the most exciting place on earth to her. But that was before she tasted Las Vegas. Now it seemed a cold, mechanical, and impersonal place. She'd never thought herself to be claustrophobic but the day of the first recording session, she wondered. Once the mike was adjusted, the headset in place, and the door of the cut-room closed, her throat seemed to close also. If it hadn't been for the friendly engineer smiling at her from the sound room, she might well have given up and quit. He reminded her of Gary McIntyre, the guy who taught her the ropes back in Tulsa, all those many years ago. Everyone called him Mac. She and Mac had become good friends. His favorite saying to her was, "Remember me when you're rich and famous!" And he always said it like he meant it.

After the first session, which she felt to be a total flop, she bucked up with new resolve. It would require even harder work and concentration than she'd imagined. No spotlights, no black sequined dress, no dancing feet, no cheers, no applause. She was totally alone in that room.

But if this was the way to gain the success needed, then she would rise above it! If it meant she must work twice as hard, then she would work twice as hard. Whatever it took, she was ready. By the final session, she was gaily bantering with the soundmen, asking them myriads of questions in order to learn how to best work with them and the equipment.

Vic was right about the computers. Extraordinary sounds came from the keyboards and the results were exciting. As they worked with her—playing back numbers after the mixing was completed—she, too, could marvel at the end result. And hearing the end result made the recording sessions easier and easier to master.

Mitzi seemed to know even before Newt or the recording company when, weeks later, the album reached the top ten on the charts. It took off faster than any of them expected or predicted. Roshelle was still in bed the morning Mitzi came dancing in, waving the trade magazines. She always read two or three and meticulously compared notes.

"We made it. We made it!" she shouted. "Rosh, wake up. You're on the top ten. Look at this."

Roshelle willed her eyes to open as Mitzi yanked open the draperies. The sprightly girl whirled around a few more times, then plopped down on Roshelle's bed. "Look here. Here it is!"

Roshelle rolled over and grabbed at the magazine. She squinted to see through blurry eyes. "Well, I'll be." There it was—number seven on the chart. She reached for the tumbler of water on the bedside table and sipped. The water soothed it temporarily but the nagging little scratchiness refused to go away. She would ask Mitzi to get her more lozenges later. Mitzi was bouncing so much that Roshelle could hardly drink or read. "Will you sit still so I can read this?"

"Sit still? How can I sit still?" She jumped to her feet and twirled around, humming the winning cut on the CD. "How can you just sit there? You're famous, Roshelle. This is what you've been waiting for. Aren't you thrilled?"

"I am thrilled, Mitzi. But I'm still not quite awake. Is there coffee?" She padded into the bathroom to splash cold water on her face. Why wasn't she more excited? Her song on the top ten. . .top in the entire nation. She had always thought that would send her into spasms of ecstasy.

"Of course there's coffee. I'll get you a cup."

"No need to bring it, Mitzi. Give me a few minutes and I'll be down."

She could hear Mitzi singing and hopping all the way down the stairs.

All of them—the people at Laurel, Newt, she, and Mitzi—had all watched the song climb on the charts, like an owner watching his horse at the Kentucky Derby. The reviews had been great since the beginning. "Brightest up-and-coming young singer," some had said. One described her voice as a "gentle, sultry mix of New York and Oklahoma." "Warm and personable," another said. Newt had already begun lining up publicity people to work on the "angles," as he called them.

Now, talks with the recording company president included discussions of the next CD *and* a music video. It was a heady thought.

Recording company president, Mr. Laurel, called that morning before she had finished her second cup of coffee and conveyed his heartiest congratulations to her. Then he invited her to a party given by another Laurel label recording artist. Roshelle wasn't sure she wanted to go but later, when she talked to Newt, he said she had no choice in the matter.

"Now, sweets, do I care if you want to go or not? The press will be there and it's high time to get your pretty mug out in the public's eye. In fact, I think we'll have Louis concoct a ravishing little outfit for the evening." He rattled off the address of Louis's Beverly Hills studio as Roshelle motioned for Mitzi to hand her a pen and some paper.

What had made her think it would always be her and the boys when she reached this point? She had never had a clear vision of herself without Benny by her side. Stupid thinking. As with the recording sessions, she had to rethink everything. But, she would do it.

Late that afternoon, when she and Mitzi returned from the fitting at Louis's, they staggered into the front door, weighted down with packages. Every time they went out, they purchased another item or two for the house.

Mitzi was busy extolling the good looks of Louis and Victor Moran. "Victor has the clear hazel, bottomless eyes that seem to look right through you. But Louis ...whew! Louis has eyes that sparkle, dance, and shine all at once. And that gorgeous hair. Mmm, all those curls." Mitzi pulled groceries out of a sack and put them up in the cupboard as Roshelle unwrapped the soapstone carvings they had picked up at a darling little shop near Louis's studio.

"Vic seems so serious and Louis is always cutting up," Mitzi went on. "Which one do you think is the better hunk, Rosh? Give me your honest opinion."

Roshelle was studying the carvings and deciding where

in her studio she would put them. She'd also purchased several new books and now she picked one up and leafed through it.

"Rosh, are you ignoring me?"

"Hmm? Why, heavens no. I'd never ignore you, Mitzi."

"That's a flat out lie. You're ignoring me now. Why don't you want to tell me who you think is the better looking guy?"

"Because it doesn't make a bit of difference what I think, that's why." The blinking light on the answering machine caught her eye and she punched the button.

It was Newt. "Hey, sweets, know of a lady by the name of Rayford? Cora Rayford, from some place called Sandott, Oklahoma? I don't know how she got my number, but she wants to talk to you. Naturally, I didn't give out your number. She says it's very important. But then, that's what they all say," he quipped, and then left the number and hung up.

Roshelle slowly sat down at the bar beside the kitchen phone. "I wonder how she tracked me down?"

Mitzi pulled her head out of the refrigerator. "Rayford? Wasn't that your name before you changed it?" She straightened up with a cantaloupe balanced in her hand. "Hey, Rosh. Is Cora Rayford your mother?"

Roshelle felt her stomach churning. She could only nod.

Mitzi came over and put her arm around Roshelle's shoulders. "Is it that bad? You look sick."

"I feel sick. Wonder what she wants?"

"Hey, I left home, too, remember. But I've gone back a few times. It didn't kill me."

"Wonder what she wants?" Roshelle repeated as though she'd not heard.

"Maybe she's ill or something. Want me to dial it?"

"I wish I never had to talk to her again ever."

"Your own mother?"

Roshelle nodded.

"She beat you or something?"

"No. It's not that simple. I'll call her from my room. Thanks, Mitzi." She felt her friend give her a squeeze and, as always, it made her want to curl up like a baby and cry, just cry until all her tears were spent. That is, if they ever could be spent. She sometimes felt she had a big enough reserve to last a lifetime.

By the time her mother's voice came on the line a few minutes later, Roshelle was in a cold sweat.

"Rachel? Well, finally. It's taken several days and a host of phone calls to find you. You'd think you could at least give us a number where we can reach you. This has caused me a great deal of trouble. Always so much trouble."

"My name's Roshelle now, Mother. Roshelle Ramone. Legally."

"I've never heard of the name Roshelle. But Rachel is a good solid Bible name. And it's the one I chose for you the day you were born."

No sense in trying to argue, she chided herself. "Newt said you needed to talk to me."

"Newt. Is that the name of the man I talked to? Your agent? What a rude man he is. Well, whether or not you care at all, I thought it was only fitting that you know. Your Uncle Jess is in the hospital. They don't expect him to live. If you want to see him again—and it's only proper that you would—you need to come home right away."

Home. What a funny word for her to use. Home. It

sounded almost like a joke. She wanted to laugh right out loud. Or did she want to laugh because Uncle Jess was finally down and almost out? She could see a little humor in that.

What should she do? It was expected of her to be there. How could she not go? As much as they all already despised her, if she didn't go, and he died, they'd have that much more to hold against her.

"I have an important party to attend Saturday night. I'll fly out early Sunday morning."

"Party? What kind of party?"

Roshelle ignored the question. The words and tone sounded no different now than when she was fifteen. "Is Uncle Jess in Tulsa?"

"That's right. In Tulsa."

"I'll be there on Sunday."

"You can't come tomorrow? The doctors aren't holding out much hope."

"Impossible. Sunday's the soonest."

"Want to give me your number so I can let you know if anything happens?"

Not a chance, she breathed inwardly. "I'll stay in touch." She quickly hung up before another word could be said.

seven

The recording company's party was a new adventure in her new life. People she'd read about, people she'd seen on TV, those whose albums she'd listened to—there they were, mingling and talking and having a great time. And she was part of it. The entire evening was like a dream.

Roshelle had finally talked Newt into serving as her escort so she wouldn't be alone. For all his tough business dealing, Newt had turned out to be a good friend. Old enough to be her father, he provided a measure of safety for her.

In his classic '58 Thunderbird, which he said he loved more than his third wife who was honestly his favorite, he drove clear across town to fetch her and take her to the home of Blaine and Gloria Bonaros in fashionable Bel Air.

Blaine was one of Laurel's long-standing recording artists. Many gold records hung on his walls. As Newt nosed the white Thunderbird up into the driveway, the guard at the gatehouse checked their identification before opening the iron gates. The driveway led them over arched stone bridges where swans and ducks glided in the quiet pools below. Small waterfalls were strategically placed here and there. Lush gardens, set about with formal hedges, banana palms, bamboo, and flowering trees of all kinds, flanked the drive.

Roshelle felt herself gasp as the house came into view. A stately mansion of English tudor style, it look as though it had been plucked up from the English countryside and set here—except for the palms, that is.

"Don't let it swoon you," Newt said with a little sniff. "They put their pants on one leg at a time just like you do."

She looked over at him and smiled.

The valet parked the car while Newt took her arm and led her to the front flagstone entryway. He handed a card to the butler at the door and they were welcomed in.

In her mind, Roshelle had tried to imagine such a house as this, but failed miserably. Now, as she walked through it, it was still beyond belief. However, rather than garish as she had expected, it was decorated with subdued colors, solid dark wood, and tasteful furniture pieces.

Sounds of laughter, conversation, and music echoed through the house, as they were led down a long hallway into a wing of the home. The room they entered was a good deal more informal than the main part of the house. Wallpaper in a soft celery green was set off with flowered borders. The light oak floors and tall, uncurtained windows gave the room an airiness, even though it was filled with a crowd of mingling party-goers.

Roshelle was sure that in the daylight not only would sunlight flood this room, but the view of all the outdoors as well. At the far end of the room, the floor raised into a platform where a combo was playing soft dance music. Through the french doors she could see several couples dancing on the lighted veranda. Past the veranda's balcony, she could see the round cupola of a garden gazebo. Perhaps one day she and Mitzi would have a place like this.

They were quickly greeted by the host and hostess, as well as by Mr. Ted Laurel himself, all of whom gave warm

welcomes and the kisses on the cheek and hugs that
Roshelle had come to expect. She was nervous as a cat.
Obviously sensing her uneasiness, Newt stayed at her
elbow and introduced her to those she didn't know.

In all her years of traveling on the road, she'd never
touched hard liquor. But, as the frosty little glasses were
being passed around, Newt handed her one and she drank
it. Sweet and cold, yet warm, it created a bubbly feeling
inside.

There was one familiar face in the crowd. Louis
Sarviano came up to say hello. His hug had a bit more
feeling than the others. "You look absolutely wonderful
tonight, Roshelle," he said, kissing her warmly on the
cheek. "But then I've never seen you when you didn't."

"You can say that because I wear your designs," she
said, wishing she didn't blush so easily.

"I was not looking at the dress, m'love," he said softly
into her ear.

He and Newt fell into talking business talk and, as they
moseyed through the crowd, Louis seemed to stay with
them.

The most glorious part of the evening came when Mr.
Laurel, who, as he told her was now to be called "Ted,"
went to the platform and stopped the party for an announcement. He motioned for Roshelle to come to where
he was standing. She wasn't sure she heard correctly in the
midst of all the clamor but, as everyone quieted, Newt
gave her a little shove.

Then, Ted Laurel, President of Laurel Recording Company, proposed a toast to their newest star. The adrenalin
rush was equal to the one she had at her closing night in
Vegas. The applause. . .the attention. Off to the side of

the room, near the tall windows, was a stunning white grand piano. Waving toward it, Ted asked her to play a few cuts from the CD. Later, she couldn't remember why she didn't want to go to the party in the first place.

After that, she was asked to dance by several of the men present who, previously, hadn't noticed her. Photographers were everywhere. "Learn to keep smiling," Newt had instructed her. And she did. She would. She would learn it all. Whatever it took, she'd do it.

Louis was also one who asked her to dance on the veranda. But, unlike the others, he had an excellent sense of rhythm. They glided together as though they had practiced for years and she found she quite enjoyed being in his arms.

"Hey, sweets, you was great tonight," Newt told her as he steered the Thunderbird up into her driveway. "Really great. They loved you. You didn't need to be scared."

"I wasn't really scared."

"Petrified?"

She giggled, feeling the effect of the drinks. "That's closer to it."

"Well, the next party that comes around, one of those handsome, hairy-legged young male creatures will be escorting you. Instead of a crusty old codger like me. They all had their eyes on you."

She giggled again. "Some real hunks, for sure."

"What time are you flying out tomorrow?" He pointed to his watch. "Correction—today."

The happy bubble burst as she suddenly recalled what lay ahead—a trip back to the past—and she was frightened. At first she had wanted Mitzi to go, too. But there were still so many details to be taken care of before the tour and before the video shoot. Newt asked that Mitzi stay here to catch up all the loose ends. It seemed the worst possible time for Roshelle to be going.

"My plane leaves at nine."

"Wish you didn't have to go now. But, family is family. This is your uncle, right?"

She nodded mutely. Her stomach was churning again. Was it too much food and too many drinks? "My father's brother."

"You gotta be true to family if you can," he said.

Right, she thought. True to family, even though family was never true to me.

Newt came around to open her door and led her up the front steps and helped her inside. Mitzi was asleep; the house was quiet.

"Hurry and go see your old uncle and get back here so we can continue the business of making you famous. . .and me rich." He gave her a little hug and planted a kiss on her forehead.

After he left, she promptly went to the bathroom off her bedroom and threw up. A gruesome way to end her gallant evening. The remainder of the night was miserable as well but she dared not take sleeping pills for fear she'd over-sleep the next morning. Sleep was fitful. There were dreams of Uncle Jess. . .and of her mother—together.

In the morning she realized she hadn't even begun to pack for the trip. Mitzi said it was because, psychologically, she was trying to avoid the thought of going.

"Right," Roshelle retorted softly so as not to disturb her aching head. "And who hired you to be my analyst?"

Mitzi was helping arrange a few things in the suitcase. "I'm everything else around here so you might as well add analyst to the list."

"Thanks a whole bunch." Roshelle was in the bathroom grabbing cosmetics and putting them in the overnight case. "Where are those lozenges we bought?"

"Down in the kitchen."

"Would you get them? I don't want to forget them."

"Your throat still sore?"

"A little."

"Hadn't you better have a doctor look at it?"

Roshelle peeked out the bathroom door. "So now we add nurse to analyst?"

"Not a chance. I'm too squeamish. When I heard you in here throwing up your shoes last night, I wouldn't have come in for anything."

"Just get the lozenges, please!"

Mitzi dropped the nightgown she was folding. "All right. All right."

The overnight bag was ready. What else would she need? How could she know what to wear when her mother disapproved of everything? She pulled open a bureau drawer and rummaged through it. Her hand hit something hard. She pulled out a book from beneath the undergarments. The Bible from the Miami hotel! She had almost forgotten about it. As she put in on the bureau, it fell open to where the first violets from Vic were pressed. The pages were stained where the little blossoms had been crushed. She ran her finger over the stain. The words she touched almost jumped out at her. Psalm 69:30. "I will praise the name of God with a song, and will magnify him with thanksgiving."

A shiver ran through her entire body. She slammed the book shut and dropped it back in the drawer.

Mitzi came bounding back into the room and tossed the package of lozenges into the suitcase. "Say, I was just thinking. Isn't Tulsa where that Victor what's-his-name is from?"

Roshelle closed the filled suitcase and picked it up. "Mitzi, my dear. Sometimes you just talk too much!"

eight

Roshelle collapsed into the seat of the Tulsa-bound plane. She was near exhaustion, having worked so hard for so many weeks. After asking the flight attendant for a pillow, she tucked it under her head, leaned against the window, and gazed out at the quiet clouds.

She should never have let herself be talked into going back. She hadn't been back since the day she packed her things and crawled out the window. Cora Rayford didn't know her daughter could climb out on the back porch roof and shin down the railings. Actually, Roshelle had done it many times. But this time it was for good. No more would she be grounded for days at a time.

She tried to picture Uncle Jess. What would she say to him? The hate for him still burned inside her. If it weren't for Uncle Jess, her father might still be alive today.

The plane droned on above the fleecy clouds. Her heavy eyelids closed and she was in the basement of the small white church in Sandott. The summer days there were so hot. She'd gone down in the basement to get cool and play . . .to get away from the summer heat. Then footsteps on the stairs. She had to move back into the shadows; she wasn't supposed to be there. Mother would be mad, maybe even use the lilac switch on her legs. She pushed her back against the cool wall behind the stacks of folding chairs.

Uncle Jess. . .it was only Uncle Jess. She started to

move, then stopped. Another voice was there in the dimness of the basement. Another voice whispering the name "Jess" over and over. And he said her name back ..."Cora." The two forms stood close, very close. She put her hands over ears to shut out the sounds of their embraces and their kisses. She didn't want to hear.

What would Daddy say? The question screamed inside her young mind. She sat very still, not moving, even though her stomach felt like she was going to be very sick.

Suddenly, Roshelle jerked her head up. The plane...she was still on the plane. She excused herself to the restroom where she could catch her breath and freshen her makeup. She let cool water run over her clammy hands. That horrid dream! She'd thought she was rid of it for good. If only she didn't have to go back.

Tulsa had grown and changed and yet was still much the same. She drove around for a time in the rental car, just looking. A new exchange on the interstate caused her to totally lose her sense of direction. But, as she drove the streets, she could still find her way around. The city was perfectly laid out in neat mile squares.

The bar where she had landed her first singing job was gone. It was now an Italian restaurant. Strange. Across town, the recording studio was still there where she had cut so many ad jingles. In fact, it appeared to have enjoyed a face lift. She smiled as she drove slowly by, remembering. Maybe some of the guys were still there who would remember her. . .like Mac. She toyed with the idea of stopping by the next day.

She chose a hotel near the hospital. If she were checked in before visiting the hospital, perhaps she wouldn't have to go out to Sandott at all.

The hotel was nice. Not the Supreme Royale, but nice. Benny would have liked it. Here she was—back in a hotel room again. But now she was really alone. From her window she could actually see the hospital. A scary feeling crept over her. She should have asked for a room on the other side of the hall.

Her mother was expecting her and she couldn't put it off. She had to go over there and face this—alone.

The tailored navy dress she'd chosen was as conservative as she could get and still be herself. A last glance in the mirror didn't give her much courage. She was ready, but she couldn't walk out that door. Why was she so filled with dread?

What if. . .? She went to the bedside table and opened the drawer. As she expected, there was a Bible. She picked it up and flipped through the pages. She remembered having a favorite verse when she was only nine years old. But where was it? And what made her think it would make any difference at this point?

But she kept flipping pages. It was in the New Testament—that much she remembered. Matthew, Mark? At the end of one of the gospels, and she remembered it was in red. Ah, there. Matthew 28:20. "And, lo, I am with you always, even unto the end of the world."

"With you always. With you always." She was in the swing in the back yard, swinging higher and higher, singing her own little song about Jesus always being with her, always. "Always" was an important word to a nine-year-old girl.

She closed the book. She couldn't explain it, but now she could walk out that door.

Hospital smells were high on Roshelle's list of least likely favorites. She was thankful that she at least had taken the time earlier for a sandwich. She slipped a lozenge in her mouth. Perhaps if she stayed over a couple of days, she could drop by one of the nearby clinics and have her throat looked at. They'd probably give her an antibiotic to get rid of this lingering infection. *And* probably tell her to rest more, and stop working so hard.

"Jess Rayford," she said to the lady dressed in pink, sitting at the information desk.

"Reverend Jess Rayford?" the lady asked.

"Yes. Reverend." Roshelle stifled a comment.

"Eighth floor. Check with the nurse at the desk. There's limited visiting."

Her mother had warned her that he was pretty bad off. But it hadn't truly registered in her mind until that moment. She stepped off the elevator at the eighth floor and the nurse at the desk wanted to know if she was a relative. She only nodded.

"To your left. Room 844."

The room was overflowing with flowers. Just as it should be for the respected pastor of the community, she thought grimly. The fragrance was like a funeral. Roshelle's palms were damp.

Her mother was there beside the bed. She looked the same—prim, proper, and in control. There was a moment before her mother detected her presence. A moment in which Roshelle let her eyes move to the bed. . .to the person lying in the bed who bore little resemblance to the harsh man who took over her life following her father's death. It was not the man who condemned her every action and word. It was not the man who seemed to take delight in making her life miserable. This was just a tired old man lying there, very close to death.

Her mother turned then and saw her. "Rachel. So you did come." She rose and came across the room to give her daughter a light hug. One would have thought they parted a few days ago, rather than several years ago.

"I said I would come."

"Yes, but. . .well, never mind. You're here. That's all that matters now." She turned back to the bed. "He's much better today. Much better. I know he might not look very well to you. You've been away for so long you don't even know what he's gone through. It's been so hard on him these past few years. But he's hanging on. Yes, sir, he's hanging on. The doctor said he'd not seen such a strong will in a long time."

She still had her hand on Roshelle's arm, but it was as though she were talking to someone across the room. "It was touch and go when we first brought him in. Had to call an ambulance to bring him here. Heart trouble. It's his heart. It was so awful. I thought sure. . .we thought he was a goner for sure."

Her mother let go of her then and moved back toward the bed. This was as much of a welcome as she was going to receive. Well, what did she expect? Ticker tape parades? After all, she was the one who left.

Her mother motioned for Roshelle to pull up another chair beside her. Dutifully, Roshelle did as she was bidden. "He won't know you," her mother said, still looking at the old man in the bed. "He's not roused since the surgery. But the doctors say he will. He will. It's just a matter of time." She smoothed the skirt of her dress. Cora Rayford always wore a dress. . .nice dresses.

"Just look at all these flowers, Rachel," she went on, waving her hand. "Everyone loves him. Everyone. The entire town is concerned. Mr. Farnum at the bank keeps asking if he can do anything. He's given me as much time off as I need."

Her mother had always hated the thought of working outside the home but, after her husband died, she had no choice. However, the bank seemed to be a proper place for a person like Cora who cared about looking proper.

"Why, I can hardly keep up with all the get well cards that have come," Cora continued.

"Why should you?" Roshelle asked.

Cora stopped short and turned to look at her daughter. "Why should I what?"

"Why should you have to keep up with the cards? Doesn't he have a secretary at the church?"

"I should have known you'd say something like that." She stood to straighten the sheets then poured water into a tumbler, even though the man in the coma would not be taking a drink any time soon. "You really aren't our dear little Rachel anymore, are you?"

"My name is Roshelle."

"Well, Roshelle, or whoever you are, we are all the family your Uncle Jess has. Why would we want to let a secretary handle things? Is that how you think of family? You just turn your back and let other people take over?"

"Might be less painful." In the room together for five minutes and already they were at one another's throats. Nothing had changed.

"Painful?" Cora pulled a tissue from the box on the bedside table and touched here eye. "You want to talk about painful? You have no idea the pain you've caused us.

Your Uncle Jess was worried sick after you ran away. I lay awake nights wondering where you were. Wondering if you were dead or alive."

"For the first year and a half, I was right here in Tulsa." She remembered the little upstairs apartment she shared with her best friend's older sister. Most nights she cried as she slept on the floor of the living room. Some nights she was afraid they would find her and take her back, other nights, afraid they wouldn't. And they didn't. Later, she learned through her friend that Uncle Jess convinced Cora not to search. "She'll come home when she gets cold and hungry," he had said.

When Roshelle heard that, it put steel into her backbone as nothing else could have. She knew she'd never go back.

"Did you expect us to go looking through every sleazy bar in Tulsa?" her mother asked sharply. "Is that what you wanted of your family?"

"It was a pretty nice bar actually. The guy who owned it was kind and bighearted. He loved the way I sang. He gave me a chance."

"There is no such thing as a nice bar. You know that. And *how* you sing has never been the problem, Rachel." She reached up and patted her graying hair. "It's *what* you sing that was always the problem. Those crude, lewd lyrics. Your Grandma Riley would be shocked if she ever heard you—"

"Let's leave Grandma out of this since she's not here to speak for herself." Roshelle vacillated between wanting to scream and wanting to cry. She stood up and stepped to the window. How could she get out of here? "So where's Janey? I thought she'd be here." Her little sister was the only one of the family she really wanted to see.

"She couldn't get a sitter. And she goes by Jane now. Even her husband calls her Jane."

"Sitter?"

Cora enjoyed playing the game to the hilt. "Of course, you wouldn't know. She's married and has a baby. Since you weren't here, she had to ask a friend to be her maid of honor at the wedding. It broke her heart. Truly broke her heart."

The door opened and a nurse pleasantly informed them that the visiting time was over. The interruption gave Roshelle a moment to savor the thought that she was now an aunt. Little Janey was actually a mother. Cute, perfect little Janey. One of the few bright spots in Roshelle's dark childhood world. In spite of the fact that all of Janey's golden qualities were constantly brought to Roshelle's attention, she still adored her younger sister.

"We'll be in the coffee shop," Cora told the nurse. "Please call us there if there's any change."

"Of course, Mrs. Rayford," the nurse answered as she drew the curtain around the bed.

The coffee shop was crowded. Roshelle was craning her neck to look in the room to see if there were any empty tables when she heard a voice from behind her down the hall, calling her. Like a call from out of her past. "Rachel. It's really you. I can't believe it. Welcome home." Her younger sister nearly knocked her over in a bear hug. Now this was a welcome. Roshelle didn't even mind the stares.

"I know it's Roshelle, but it'll take me a while to get onto that." Janey stepped back to look. "You're beautiful! Just like I knew you'd be."

"Hi, Janey. Thanks." But it was Janey who was

beautiful. Tall and slender like their father. Dark shiny hair like his. And the doelike eyes. "You grew up while I had my back turned," Roshelle told her.

"I want you to know I've missed you," Janey said, her eyes misting.

"I've missed you, too." She grabbed Janey's hand. "But Mother said you couldn't come this afternoon."

"When I found out you were coming, I took Darla to Al's mother's and came as soon as I could. I wouldn't have missed seeing you for the world."

"We're blocking the doorway, girls," Cora said in her usual curt manner. "Let's get through the line and find a place to sit down."

"Darla?"

"My baby girl. You've got to see her, Rachel. Roshelle," she corrected herself.

"Some of my friends call me Rosh."

"Rosh? I like that. Can you come out and see our place? Meet Alex and see our baby? Your little niece?"

"Out where?"

"Girls, please. We can talk at the table."

Janey pulled Roshelle over to the deli counter. They ordered premade sandwiches and coffee. "We have a house in Sandott."

When Roshelle heard the town's name her heart sunk. She shook her head. "I don't know, Janey. There's so much going on. I've got to get back as soon as possible."

They sat down at a small table by the windows. It was as if Cora were not there.

"I'd bring her to you, but when I go to see Uncle Jess—"

"What does she look like?" Roshelle wanted to know.

"Beautiful, of course." She opened her purse and pulled out a little album full of snapshots. Janey and Alex and the baby. In a little house in Sandott, Oklahoma. So cozy. And she seemed content. Unaffected Janey. Like Mitzi, she was always so unaffected.

Roshelle wondered why she couldn't be the same way. But she wasn't. There was no use pretending. This place affected her. In the worst way.

"You cut a CD, didn't you?" Janey said when the photos were put away.

Roshelle nodded. She heard Cora clear her throat in disgust.

"I've been watching for it. I knew it would come. Sooner or later, I knew it would. Just like you always said you would." Was that admiration in her sister's eyes? "Now one song is climbing, right?"

Roshelle pulled the wrapping from the sandwich that looked a trifle squashed. "We just learned that it's in the top ten."

"Jane Rayford," Cora butted in. "Are you listening to—"

"Ingram, Mother. The name's Ingram. You were at the wedding remember?" She smiled kindly at Cora and turned back to Roshelle. "Top ten? In the nation?" She threw her head back. "Can you believe this? My own sister. So where are the photographers and news reporters?" She fluffed her curly hair, and glanced over her shoulder. "Are we being watched? Will I be interviewed in one of those tabloids?"

Cora let her spoon clatter into the saucer by her coffee cup. "Well, I should hope not. Haven't we had humiliation enough with this skeleton in our closet?"

Roshelle recoiled, but Janey remained cool. With a pat on Roshelle's arm, she said, "And this is only the beginning. I'm so proud of you. Al and I pray for you every day."

Praying for her? To succeed? She covered her sister's hand with her own. "Thanks, Janey. I appreciate that." And she meant it. Janey seemed to make the other unbearable things fade into the background.

nine

The clinic was down the street from the hospital, a few blocks from the hotel. Bright lavender, purple, and yellow pansies in the clinic flower beds bobbed their heads in the morning breeze. This was a perfect opportunity to take the time to get this sore throat taken care of. There was never enough time in California when she had so many deadlines to face.

She called first thing that morning and the appointment was set for ten. Her wait was brief. Dr. Beasley was a gray-haired, friendly man with full cheeks and wire-rimmed glasses. An ears, nose, throat specialist, she was told. He did all the normal, noncommittal "hmm-ing" that doctors always do when they look at you.

"I know I've been overworking," she confessed to his unspoken questions. "I know I probably should rest more. But there's never enough time."

He nodded and looked a little more. "We'll do a couple of tests. How long will you be in town?"

"I'm not sure. I have to get back as soon as possible." Honestly, she didn't know how she could stay another minute. Janey kept begging her to drive out to visit their "place" and Roshelle was running out of excuses why she couldn't.

"If I get the reports back this afternoon, where can I contact you?" he asked.

He scribbled as she gave him the hotel name and her

room number. "Since you're here temporarily, I'll ask them to hurry on this."

"Is it strep?" She'd heard awful things about strep throat. It must be more than just an infection or he would have said something.

"I'll call you as soon as we know."

Why can't they just tell a person what's wrong? she wondered as she drove out into the busy traffic. It was unnerving to be left hanging. She turned in the direction of the recording studio. It would be fun to go back and look around. To remember those early days. RIGHT ON TRACK RECORDING STUDIO the sign read. It was the same sign. She used to ride the bus out here when she had scheduled sessions and Mac would sometimes drive her home. All the guys were kind to her. Just like the guys in the band. She shook her head. No sense in thinking about the band again. It only made her depressed and sad.

The business office was done in tones of mauve and violet—restful and inviting. "I'm looking for an engineer by the name of Gary McIntyre," she said to the young receptionist.

The girl reached for the phone. "Can I give him your name?"

"You mean Mac's really here?" She felt like laughing.

The girl gave a questioning look as she picked up the phone. "He's back there. Your name, please?"

"Just say 'an old friend.'" This was too good to be true. She'd never dared hope he'd still be around. Maybe some of the other guys were, too.

"Gary," the girl was saying. "Someone to see you. An 'old friend.'" There was a touch of sarcasm in the tone, but Roshelle didn't mind.

The side door to the office opened. "Naw. Tell me I'm dreaming. I don't believe this." The barrel-chested Mac gave a throaty laugh and grabbed her in an unrestrained hug as the receptionist watched. "Our little Rachel. Only not so little." He stepped back and took a look. "Whew, not so little. Big star now, eh?"

"Well, I'm getting there."

"We knew you would. We all knew you would. Come on back. I don't have another client for a while." He guided her through the door back to one of the studio control rooms. His domain. "Hold the calls," he said over his shoulder to the receptionist. "When I first saw your photo on the album I knew Roshelle was you. I'm so happy for you."

"Thanks." He was rooting for her and he'd noticed the new album. It made her feel great.

"What in the world would ever bring you back to Tulsa?"

"An emergency. My uncle is ill."

"You're in touch with your family?" Mac was well aware of her home situation.

"I am now."

"You don't sound too happy about it."

She tucked a strand of hair behind her ear and perched herself on the stool he pulled up. She gave a little sigh, not knowing how to answer. "It was a bad time to leave L.A., and. . .well, nothing has changed here." She brightened. "Except I find out I'm an aunt. My kid sister got married and has a little girl."

Mac gave a wide grin. "I'm married, too." He pulled out his wallet and showed the typical family photo—

lovely wife and two darling toddlers. "She's the greatest," he declared pointing at the photo for emphasis. "Best thing that ever happened to me."

She made the necessary polite remarks. All these happily married people were making her nervous. She looked around at the control room. "The place looks great. You're staying right on top of all the latest technology, I see." She patted a nearby computer console.

"Can't afford not to. We're doing big things in here now. Some pretty important people pass through these doors. And the videos. You should see our videos, Rachel. You'd be impressed."

"Roshelle."

"Oh yeah, Roshelle. Pretty name."

"I'm already impressed. I'm impressed that you're still hanging around here."

He straightened. "I've outlasted all the guys you knew, plus three owners. Can you believe that? Three owners. I sort of come with the furniture." He chuckled at his own joke.

Roshelle gazed through the soundproof window to the cut room where she had recorded ad jingles, all the while dreaming she was cutting her own album. Now that dream had come true.

"The newest owner has some bucks," he went on. "This is actually his second studio in town. Has an office in the Clancy Towers building."

"Mmm. Sounds like he does have a few bucks. You better be nice to this one."

"Hey, this is the easiest guy to be nice to you ever saw. Great to work with and knows this business inside out and upside down."

"Really," she answered absently. Time was getting by and her mother expected her back at the hospital within the hour.

"At one time he owned big casinos in Miami. Worked with all the big name stars."

"Miami. Right. And then he worked his way up to this recording studio in Tulsa. That makes a lot of sense." She couldn't keep the sarcasm out of her voice. "Why would anyone leave Miami for this?"

Mac ducked his head. "He got saved."

"He got what?"

"Gave his life to the Lord. Changed him completely."

"Is this guy. . .?" But the question was never finished. From the control room window she saw the door from the reception area open. There stood Vic. She felt the color drain from her face.

Mac jumped up. "There's Vic now. You'll have to meet him."

There was no back door, no escape route, no way out. Vic's expression was a combination of surprise and sheer delight as he saw her standing there.

Mac stepped to the door and motioned to Vic. "Hey, bossman. There's someone here I'd like you to meet."

Vic strode down the hall toward them. "Roshelle. What a pleasant surprise."

"Hello, Vic."

Mac's hands dropped at his side. "You two know each other?" He slapped his forehead. "I should have known. Victor Moran, you know everybody! But I bet you didn't know little Rachel here, I mean Roshelle, recorded her first songs in this cut room."

"I had no idea. But I'm pleased."

"I've got to be going." Roshelle felt cornered. She never dreamed she'd see him here. "I'm expected at the hospital."

Vic's face registered his disappointment. "You just got here and now you have to leave."

"I just dropped by to take a look. Curiosity. The place looks great." She moved toward the door. Past Vic. He reached out his hand. She didn't take it.

"How long will you be here? A few days?"

"I have to get back to L.A. soon. Newt's scheduling a tour and we hope to squeeze in the video filming before that. There's so much to do." She successfully moved past him into the hall.

"Let me give you my home phone number and my pager number. If you have a minute before you leave, let's get together." He pulled a card from his pocket and wrote on the back and handed it to her.

She slipped it into her purse. "Bye, Mac." She gave a little wave. "It was great to see you again. Thanks."

"You're welcome here anytime, Roshelle. Congratulations on your success—and all the successes to come. I know there'll be many."

Mac stayed in the control room, but Vic walked her through the reception area and out into the parking lot to her car. "So this is the studio where you got your start."

"If you can call car dealership ad jingles a beginning."

"To paraphrase Zechariah, four and ten, don't despise the day of small things." He opened the car door for her. "Everyone has to begin somewhere. I came to Tulsa almost like you did—with very little. But the Lord has blessed me."

She slipped into the hot car, turned the key, and cranked

up the air conditioner. "I guess I'll see you around. We seem to have a way of running into one another."

He gave his slow smile. "We do, don't we? Don't forget. Call me if you have a minute. Call me if you need anything."

She nodded and pulled the door closed.

Uncle Jess's condition was unchanged. The room was the same as the day before. Her mother looked the same, but in a different dress. Cora held a devotion booklet in her hand. It appeared she had been reading to Uncle Jess before Roshelle's arrival. The room was close and depressing. Some of the flowers were wilting.

She looked at her uncle's pale quiet face and tried to remember how animated the face had been as he slammed his fist on the pulpit and preached hellfire and damnation to his attentive congregation. Or how angry he had looked when he reprimanded her. She remembered his coarse, loud voice. Never gentle. Never quiet. But that must have been another person. Not this old man lying here sick. It was difficult to sort out all the tangled threads of memories. There were knots and snarls all through it.

"How is he?" she asked politely as she came in and sat down.

"Stable, the doctor says. He seems to be out of danger now. He roused a bit in the night."

"Will Janey be coming later?" she wanted to know.

"Her name is Jane. She said she thought you were driving out to see her this evening."

"I never said that," she defended herself. Odd that it was acceptable for Janey to change her name, but not for Roshelle to change hers. But, that's the way it always had been. Janey, the sweet one, the good one, the right one. And yet the two sisters had loved one another in spite of it all. Now that's what Roshelle called a miracle.

"Alex said they were going to have a barbecue in the back yard in your honor, and having a few friends over. Grilling steaks, I believe he said."

Roshelle felt her face flush with anger. Her mother was probably at the bottom of this. She'd call Janey when she got back to her hotel room. Between the two of them maybe they could get it straightened out. "There's no way I can—"

Her mother looked at her sternly. "I would think it's the least you could do for your sister, since you weren't even with her for her wedding or the birth of her first child."

"I'm sure there are sisters the world over who have been unable to be together for every occasion, but it doesn't cause a major disaster in the family."

"Unpreventable separations are quite different from this situation. It's quite clear you could have been here had you really wanted to be. But you preferred your wild life to family."

Cora had such an uncanny way of heaping on the guilt. Nothing Roshelle said in her own defense made any difference. Rather, her defenses seemed to open the door for her mother to further condemn. It was hopeless.

She thought about that a moment as she listened to her uncle's steady, but labored breathing. It really *was* hopeless. She was stupid to stay here. For the first time, she admitted the truth—that she had come here with a measure of hope that there could be a reconciliation. How foolish she'd been.

She stood to her feet. "I'll be going now," she said

evenly.

Her mother barely glanced at her. "Sit down. You just got here."

"I have some things to take care of."

"Things that are more important than family, obviously. But then that's how it's always been with you, Rachel. Thinking of yourself first. Family never meant a thing to you."

Roshelle felt the twinge of pain as she bit into her bottom lip. She turned and walked out of the room.

ten

There were two messages at the hotel desk: one from Janey and one from Dr. Beasley. She'd call the doctor first. That was the more important thing. Now she could get the needed prescription and some relief from the pain. No reason to go up to her room since she would have to go out to pick up the prescription anyway. She made the call from the lobby phone.

"Oh yes, Miss Ramone. I'm glad we caught you before you left town. Are you nearby?"

"At the hotel."

"Good. Could you come back by the clinic? I'd like to talk to you. How about half past two?"

She felt her nerves go taut. This was strange. Doctors are busy people. They don't have time for chitchat. What was the matter? She wanted to ask him why, but she was afraid to ask. "I can be there."

"Super." Was his voice overly friendly? Just her wild imagination. "I'll see you then."

There was nowhere to go to kill the next thirty minutes so she went to her room and paced. She turned on the television and quickly vetoed that idea as she snapped it back off again. If she were home, she could be pounding out her emotions on the piano. As she paced, she hummed, then sang the lyrics of her newest song. It was a great love ballad. Perhaps with Newt on her side, she could talk Mr. Laurel into using it on her next album.

She would also talk to Newt about calling Benny and the boys off their tour so they could join her as she began her nationwide tour. She made herself dwell on every happy, exciting thing she could possibly think of. She changed out of her slacks back into the navy dress she'd worn Sunday afternoon. Then it was time to go to the clinic—alone again.

"You're a singer, right?" Dr. Beasley asked as he ushered her to a chair in his office.

"I'm a singer. A professional singer. Recording artist. Stage star. You name it. And I'll be a better singer as soon as I get this sore throat cleared up. Can you help me or not?"

"Are you singing on a regular basis at this time?"

"Is singing almost every night considered regular?"

Dr. Beasley nodded. "I think so. In a smoke-filled atmosphere?"

"You hardly ask patrons in a Las Vegas casino not to smoke."

"No, I suppose not."

She waited impatiently, wishing he would get to the point.

"Miss Ramone, I'm afraid this problem is not going to just 'clear up.' I've detected nodules on your vocal chords."

A dark silence hung between them momentarily. She tried to clear her throat and the pain there suddenly intensified. "Nodules? Like growths?"

"Yes, like little growths." His voice was calm, steady. "We see this many times in singers who abuse their voices."

"But I don't abuse my voice!" she protested. "I'm just singing. Is there anything wrong with that? I love to sing. Singing is my whole life." First her mother, and now this. She felt the anger smoldering. It wasn't fair.

"Miss Ramone, please. I'm not accusing you. I'm trying to explain—"

"Explain what? What are you telling me? What does this mean?"

"First of all, you'll need to give your voice a rest. Stop singing for a time."

"That's impossible," she snapped.

"Next," he said, ignoring her answer, "I recommend surgery to have the nodules removed."

No. This couldn't be happening to her. Surgery. Someone cutting on her throat. She couldn't bear the thought. No. She fished a tissue from her purse.

"Even with surgery we cannot guarantee that your vocal chords will be normal. But, without surgery, the problem could grow much worse."

Why was she sitting here hundreds of miles from people who cared about her? Alone. Always alone. Benny on one coast, Mitzi on the other. No one here to help. No one. She pulled herself together. She'd survived before. She'd survive again. Somewhere deep within her was that resolve. That stage smile. "Do you have a physician you want me to contact in Los Angeles? Miss Ramone? I said, do you have—"

"No. I've not been to a doctor in years. I'm so healthy. I've always been healthy. Never sick."

"Perhaps you'd like to schedule the surgery here." He nodded in the general direction of the hospital. The hospital where her uncle now lay near death. "We have excellent facilities here. You'd be well taken care of."

Roshelle straightened her shoulders, squeezing the soft tissue in her hand. "Thank you, Dr. Beasley. I'll be in touch with you if I decide to have the surgery done here in Tulsa." She stood on unsteady legs.

"Please do that. But don't wait too long. Meanwhile I'll give you a prescription that will ease the discomfort to some degree." He scratched out the note and handed it to her. "This should help. And, with proper rest, you should be fine."

"If the surgery is not done?"

"Worst case scenario?"

She drew in a breath. "Yes."

"If the nodules are malignant, the cancer could spread." He shook his head. "You don't want to take that chance."

Later, she wasn't sure how long she'd been driving around the city. Her mind was encased in a gray fog and nothing was clear. She stopped at a small park where children were playing on the swings and jungle gym. The heat assaulted her as she stepped out of the air-conditioned car, but she was oblivious to it.

The park was resplendent with dark green cedars, sprawling magnolias, and shady maples and oaks. She strolled among the trees that shaded her from the hot afternoon sun. Squirrels looked at her quizzically, then chittered and scampered away. The blue jays scolded and dive-bombed the squirrels.

In the midst of a cluster of trees was a green, wrought-iron bench. She made her way to the bench and sat down slowly. A lemony fragrance wafted down off the waxy white blossoms of the magnolia. Their beauty and serenity seemed to mock the utter confusion and turmoil in her brain.

It wasn't fair. Why should life play this cruel trick on her? "God, if You're punishing me, You've sure picked a stinky way to do it," she muttered.

From high above her, she could hear a mockingbird singing. She craned her neck to find him. There he was, atop a cedar tree, on the topmost, tiniest branch of the tree. Towering above all other surrounding trees. The branch looked much too fragile to hold the bird. But he didn't care. Nor did he care if there was, or was not, an audience to hear his lovely music. He simply sang.

"That's me," she whispered as she watched the small bird. "That's me. I'll sit on that topmost tiny frail branch. I don't care if it breaks. I don't even care if I fall. I don't care about anything except my singing. You and me, Mr. Mocker. We'll just sing our hearts out as long as we can. I'll sing till I drop."

It was growing dark when she found herself back in the hotel parking lot. She dreaded going back to an empty hotel room. As she opened her purse to pull out the room key, Vic's card tumbled out on the floor. She stooped to pick it up. "Call if you need anything," he had said.

"We'll see if Mister Christian really meant what he said," she said to herself as she headed to the lobby phone. "Or was he blowing hot air?"

The moment he heard her voice, Vic said, "Great. You've changed your mind. Can I meet you at the hotel? I'll be right over. Wait in the lobby."

His eagerness was a bit overwhelming, but she waited. She could see him as he parked out front then walked into the building. He walked with purpose and determination. One might label him as a young executive who knows where he's going. He was wearing a cool-looking print shirt with casual slacks. There was always an impeccable look about him, whether he was in a suit or not.

For a moment he stood glancing about the vast lobby area. When he saw her, his face lit up and he quickly stepped toward her. She ignored the flutter of excitement she felt at seeing him again. She didn't dare *feel* anything right now.

He reached out his hand to where she was sitting on one of the plush lobby couches. This time she took his hand, and let him help her to her feet. "Thanks for calling," he said.

"I had sort of a change in plans. I found I did have a little free time after all."

"I'm glad. Have you eaten?"

She shook her head wondering if she could eat now that she knew why her throat bothered her so. Part of her wished she'd never learned the truth. Ignorance could be bliss, after all.

He took her to a quiet restaurant, a place like she expected he would patronize. Nothing raucous.

"How's your uncle?" he asked as they were seated.

"Stable, is what the doctors say."

"Was he ill long?"

"I haven't any idea. I'm not in contact with my family."

"I'm sorry to hear that."

"Don't be. It's much better this way." She thought of her mother again. "Much better."

The waitress interrupted as she took their order. Vic ordered prime sirloin with tomato sauce but Roshelle wanted only soup and salad.

Changing the subject, he said, "Mac tells me you left home before you ever graduated from high school."

She felt her face flush. "Did he tell all my secrets? I hope he told you I took the GED and received my diploma before I was seventeen."

"Actually, I couldn't get much out of him at all. He seems rather protective of you."

She smiled thinking of Vic prying to find out more about her. Then she wondered why he would even care to know. "As my mother would say, I ran away—straight into a world of sin."

"Mac said you only wanted to sing."

Unexpected tears burned in her eyes as she nodded. "Singing was all I ever wanted. Even now."

He reached out to take her hand, but she pulled it back. "Are you all right?"

"It's been a rather emotional trip for me. I'll be all right." She struggled to regain her composure. She didn't need him feeling sorry for her. "I wanted to sing, but my family never understood. My uncle constantly preached about the sin of singing demonic lyrics."

"That must have been hard on you as a kid. Preached? You mean, he's a preacher?"

"That's what he calls himself. I have other names."

"You attended his church, I take it?"

"Most of my life."

The food was brought to the table and, as he had done the day of their picnic, Vic insisted on blessing the food— out loud. Roshelle's first reaction was embarrassment. But the sound of his voice in simple prayer had a quieting effect on her.

"What about your father? How does he fit into the picture?" he asked after he was finished with the prayer.

"Daddy," she said. "Well, Daddy's hard to describe." She was hedging. She'd not talked about her father to anyone for so many years. "He died suddenly when I was only nine."

"I'm sorry. Was it hard on you?"

"Devastating. He was my ally."

"Against whom?"

"Mother mostly." She studied his reaction to this and waited for a retort. But he quietly soaked in the information with no comment.

"What was he like?"

"Quiet. Kind." Sort of like you, she wanted to say. The thought startled her. She pretended to be concentrating on cutting a cherry tomato. Then she added, "Never condemning. Never argumentative."

He started to ask another question, but she interrupted him. That was enough. "But what about your family?" she asked quickly, to steer him away from more questions.

"No preachers, that's for sure."

"Lucky you."

"There's probably room for discussion there, but I'll let it pass," he said with a smile. "My father was into money and business and all the trappings. And my very materialistic-minded mother prodded him on. There's plenty of money in Miami real estate. And I followed right in his footsteps."

"And Mac informed on you, too. He said you owned a couple of Miami night spots. You actually *owned* them?"

He nodded and smiled. "That I did. Or they owned me."

"Either way would be fine with me."

"I thought so, too, for a while."

She wanted to know what happened. How he came to throw it all away and move to Tulsa. But, on the other hand, she didn't want to hear some preachy story about how he saw the error of his ways. Boring, boring. "So you grew up around Miami?" That would keep the conversation safe, she thought smugly.

"West Palm Beach for several years, then Miami."

"Don't you miss the wonderful beaches and the water? How can you stand being a landlocked Okie?"

This brought a chuckle. "You've hit a soft spot. I do miss the ocean a great deal. But I travel, so I try to fit in a day at the beach whenever I'm close to one, such as the one at the lake," he added, referring to the day of their picnic.

She didn't want to talk about that day, either. "So why would you choose Tulsa for a base for your recording company? You could live on either coast."

"That's the point. I travel from coast to coast so often that being situated in the center is ideal. The recording industry is doing well here. No big union problems."

She nodded. Everyone in the industry understood the strong unions in Los Angeles.

"Plus the fact that I like it here. It's a nice city."

Ugh, she thought silently. She couldn't wait to get out of here and back to L.A.

After dinner, he drove to the river and they walked out on the pedestrian bridge. Luckily, the water was up, otherwise the smell of fish would have been overwhelming.

"The nearest thing Tulsa has to a beach," she remarked as they looked out across the water. She remembered the night she strolled out on the beach alone. How clean and beautiful it was. How good it smelled.

She had let Vic take her by the hand as they walked up the stairs and across the street bridge then down again to the river bridge. Now that they were stopped midway on the bridge, she didn't try to pull away. It was as though she needed to hold onto someone. . .something. . .to try to forget what Dr. Beasley had told her that afternoon.

The bridge was almost deserted. "Monday night is definitely not the most popular night at River Parks," he commented, not looking for an answer.

Monday. It was still only Monday. She gazed out at the shimmering lights reflected on the water. Saturday night at the party seemed ages ago. A soft breeze had come up and there were flashes of lightning off to the south.

"Maybe it'll rain tonight," he said, pointing at the pink lightning.

"Could be heat lightning. With not a drop of rain."

"Heat lightning? What's that?"

She looked at him. His face was softened in the moonlight. "I forget you're not from here. Sometimes in the summer, when it's the hottest, flashes of lightning will flare up, but there's no rain. Daddy used to say those clouds were the 'empties.' It can drive a farmer batty if he's needing a good summer rain."

He looked back out across the water at the clouds. "Hmm. Fascinating. God's handiwork. I marvel at all His creations. The water, the trees, the flowers, the birds, the animals."

Now her hand was enclosed in both of his. He turned to look at her again. "And you. You are one of God's lovely creations. He created such beauty in you, Roshelle, and in your marvelous silken voice."

He brought her hand to his lips and softly kissed it. Then his arms were around her pulling her gently to him. She could sense his warmth, his tenderness. Softly he kissed her cheeks, caressed her hair, and held her close. A passion welled up in her like nothing she'd ever known before. Confusing her.

He lifted her chin and kissed her firmly on the lips. She was enraptured as she eagerly returned his kiss, inhaling his clean sweet aroma. The opposition she'd so carefully built up against this man was melting away in a matter of moments.

She caught her breath and pulled away, fighting to regain her composure. Her heart was thundering. She wanted to push him away, but she was fearful her legs would not hold her.

"Your hair glows in the moonlight," he whispered as he ran his fingers through it. "Silky. Like the silken sounds of your beautiful singing."

Now she was able to step back from him. "I think I'd better get back. Doesn't the park close soon?"

He glanced at his watch. "You're right. We're about to break curfew." Quietly, he put his arm around her, gently cradling her shoulders as walked her back to his car.

Both spoke little as he drove from River Parks to her hotel. But when he stopped the car out front, he paused before getting out. "Roshelle, there's something troubling you. Something deep inside. Is there anything I can do?"

She stiffened. How could he possibly know? No one could know. She'd already decided it would be her secret to keep. There was no need to tell anyone. "I've already said I have a few family problems," she said quickly. Send out a decoy to keep him off track. "This trip—coming here—has been difficult."

He wasn't buying it. "No one has a perfect family. I sense it's something deeper."

"There's nothing." She had to find her stage personality. The stage smile. But it was almost impossible—after his kisses and his embrace.

He reached across the car to take her hand. "Please promise me—" he started.

"I'm not real good on keeping promises," she quipped lightly. "I think I've broken almost every one I've ever made."

He ignored her. "Please promise me, if I can ever be of help, that you'll call me." He squeezed her hand. "And meanwhile, whatever it is, I'll be praying for you."

She pulled her hand away. "I'll try to keep that in mind." Why did he have to be so persistent?

He stayed close by her side as he walked her into the hotel. Stepping inside the heavy front door, Roshelle was shocked to see her mother sitting there in the lobby.

Cora rose to her feet and walked toward them, disapproval and disdain written clearly on her face. "It's about time you showed up."

eleven

"Mother. What are you doing here?"

Cora didn't bother to give Vic a glance, but glared at Roshelle. "Your uncle almost dies, and you're out gadding about town. I've been looking for you since late this afternoon." She pointed to her watch for emphasis. It was nearly midnight.

"You have no right—"

"Plus Jane was devastated when you didn't show up for supper at her house. She'd invited friends in and was so disappointed. She spent the evening crying her eyes out because you hurt her so. Have you no feelings at all?"

Janey's phone message from this afternoon. Roshelle had forgotten all about it after she talked to Dr. Beasley. Poor Janey. "How's Uncle Jess now?"

"For all that you care, he pulled through. He took a turn for the worse just after you left. It was probably the bad spirits you bring in with you. I tried to call you to let you know, but you were nowhere to be found. Obviously, you had better things to do than to be concerned about your uncle. After all he's done for you."

"All he's done for me?" Suddenly, anger was smoldering inside her like a rumbling volcano. "All he has done for *me*? Please, please tell me what that could be." She felt her body trembling. Vic moved to take her arm, but she shook him off. "What did that wretched, hateful man ever do for me? Please tell me. I'm consumed with suspense. If he dies in the next five minutes, I will not have lost a thing!"

"Rachel, your attitude is despicable," Cora said in a controlled icy tone. That was always her ploy when Roshelle lived at home—to rouse her to a state of fury, then to act calm and shocked. "You never could hold your temper, Rachel. Always flying off the handle."

Roshelle's voice was loud. People were looking, but she no longer cared. The volcano was spilling over. It was hot and it was terrible. "I tell you what. I'll take my bad spirits, my despicable attitude, and my rotten temper to where you never have to worry about them again. Now, please get out of my sight."

For the first time, Cora looked up at Vic, but said nothing. She looked back at Roshelle. "Your uncle was right about you all along."

Roshelle clenched her fists to keep from clawing and slapping. "Get away from me."

She watched as her mother walked out with her head held high. When she was out of sight, Roshelle stumbled to a nearby couch. Vic took her arm and assisted her.

She sat there stunned, willing her eyes not to shed the tears that were stinging there. She would not let that woman make her cry one more time.

"Not a pretty sight, huh, Mr. Moran?" she mumbled. "And you ask me if something's wrong?" She gave a dry laugh.

"Roshelle," Vic said softly, "you can't let this awful hatred and bitterness continue to build. It'll eat you alive."

"Right. So show me the switch and I'll sure be glad to shut it off."

"The Lord can help you to forgive. To release it. To

unload that weight of guilt."

She scooted over away from him. She should have known that, sooner or later, he would start preaching. Guilt, he says, as though she were the guilty one.

"Proverbs says we are not to despise our mothers when they are old. I had to use that verse myself so I know—"

"You don't know anything. Nothing at all. You think you can slap a little Scripture on me like a bandage and it will make everything all right?" She jumped up. "You're no different than she is." She waved in the direction where Cora walked out. "I don't need your phony, plastic religion. For once, Mr. Self-righteous, the perfect Christian doesn't have all the answers. And this time God Himself doesn't have any answers for what's troubling me."

She didn't bother to wait for the elevator, but ran up the service stairs. She was breathless when she reached her room. Quickly she packed her bags and called for the airport shuttle. There were regular flights to Dallas. She'd worry about connections to L.A. after landing in Dallas. By then, she'd be far away from this horrid place—forever!

The DFW airport was fairly empty in the wee hours of the morning. As soon as her flight to L.A. was confirmed, she called Mitzi, awakening her. The sound of her friend's voice was like a refreshing breeze blowing into her cluttered mind. Mitzi could get awake quicker than any other person she'd ever known.

After Roshelle told her the flight number and time of her arrival, Mitzi said, "Newt will be so glad you're coming back this soon. Mr. Laurel, too. They're already talking about shooting sites for the video."

"I'm ready."

"Sure was a short stay. Did everything go all right?"

"As good as could be expected."

"That bad, huh?" Mitzi could see right through her.

"Pretty bad."

"How's old Uncle Jess?"

"I don't know. And I'm not sure I even care."

"It really *was* bad."

"What about the tour? Are the details being hammered out?"

"Hammered is a good word. What a ton of work. I'm not sure who's on the phone the most, Newt or me."

Roshelle was amazed at how well Mitzi had taken the reins of the business matters. "Has Newt contacted Benny yet?"

"We're not that far into negotiations."

"Have him hold off. I need time to sort things out."

There was momentary silence on the other end. "I thought this was the moment you'd been waiting for, Rosh. The moment when the band could be—"

"I know, I know. I can't go into it now, Mitzi. We'll talk when I get there. Okay?"

"Okay. Whatever you say. I'll be at the airport to pick you up."

"Mitzi? Thanks for everything you've done. Everything you do!"

"Hey! You know it's only because there's no one else dumb enough to get mixed up in this zoo." She gave her silly laugh and was gone.

Roshelle bought an entertainment magazine and a cup of coffee and sat down to wait. She preferred the empty airport to the lonely hotel room back in Tulsa.

She flipped through the pages, looking for people she knew. People she'd met on the road, in Las Vegas, and now in L.A. She sucked in a little gasp as she saw her own picture on one of the back pages. It was only a blurb, but there it was. In a few paragraphs, it explained in detail that she was from a small town in Oklahoma and that she had run away from home at an early age. She'd never tried to hide anything, but it was uncanny how they could dig into a person's past and publish it across the country. Someone at the party last Saturday night had told her, "Don't worry when they write what's true about you, worry when they start writing things that aren't true."

Maybe Janey was right. Maybe they would track down her family in Sandott. Wouldn't Cora have a fit? Roshelle couldn't help but smile just thinking about it.

But now Janey and Alex—that was another matter. She never wanted to hurt Janey. But she guessed she already had without even trying. She had failed to call her sister back and clear up the plans for last evening.

She could hear her mother telling Janey, "Rachel would rather go out on the town with a man than spend an evening with her own sister." Or to be more correct her mother would say, ". . .than to spend an evening with her own family."

But that wasn't true. If she'd had a few minutes alone with Janey, she could have explained. Well, not explained totally, but partially. That she couldn't bear to go back to the town of Sandott—ever.

When she got back to L.A., maybe she could call Janey's house. Or even write a little note of apology. But then, with Cora always telling her side of the story, what good would it do? It was useless for Roshelle to try to justify herself or to make lame excuses. And she was weary of doing so.

When the pilot announced they were descending for entry into Los Angeles, Roshelle experienced a new rush of joy. She had everything planned out and she'd rehearsed it along the way. There was no way she could now travel with the band. That was a given.

Benny knew her too well. After one performance, he'd know something was wrong. Correction. After one short rehearsal, he'd know. As soon as Benny found out she'd been told to rest her voice, there would be no more singing. She knew that much for sure. Benny could be very persuasive. But quitting was exactly what she refused to do. She would never quit.

For her, to sing was to live. If she had no more voice, she'd just as soon leave this old world. "I'll sing till I drop," she muttered to herself as she pulled her carry-on out of the overhead compartment.

Sure, Benny would be upset at first that she didn't bring them on board, but he'd get over it. Just like she got over his not coming to be with her in Vegas. That's the way things were in this business, tough for everybody. A person just had to make do.

Mitzi was there at the terminal gate, waiting. Reliable Mitzi. Roshelle gave her a hug. "It's great to be home."

"You were gone only a couple of days."

"Are you sure? It feels like a couple of years," she said. And it had. "Plus the fact that it's great to have a home to come home to."

Mitzi laughed. "You might not be so glad when you see

how much has to be done in so short a time."

But she was glad. She wanted to fill every minute of every day so full that she would be exhausted every night. And then sleep like a baby. "What's first on the agenda?"

Mitzi, who now had her driver's license, was weaving through the dense L.A. traffic like a pro. "Newt wants to see you as soon as you get unpacked."

"That I can do."

"He has several fitting sessions set up with Louis for your outfits for the video. He has that agenda at his office. I can't remember when they're all scheduled."

"Filming isn't like stepping into a cut room, is it? Where I can wear my old grungies." A surge of excitement shot through her, as she thought of the upcoming video.

"No. Not like that at all." Mitzi glanced over at her and smiled. "So how was Oklahoma?"

"The same."

"I'm sorry. Sorry it was hard on you. Was your uncle better?"

"This is crazy, but I was never sure. I guess I should have talked to the doctors myself. But I kept taking my mother's word for everything. And I can't always believe her. Anyway, he never roused. Never even knew I was there. It was useless to go. I wish I'd never let her bully me into going in the first place."

"Did you see Mr. What's-his-name with the violets?"

"Actually, I did."

"You're kidding." Mitzi almost drove off the road. "Are you kidding me?"

"I am not kidding."

"Boy, I guess what they say about a small world is really true. Where was he?"

"I stopped by the old recording studio where I first started singing umpteen years ago and, lo and behold, he is now the owner of the place. And he walked right in while I was there."

"Blow me down."

"I agree." Blown down and blown away, Roshelle thought to herself. She had already planned how much she was going to tell Mitzi. So much and no more. Enough to be safe. No need to tell her about the dinner. About the kiss on the river bridge that still burned fresh in her memory. About the argument with her mother. Or the anger she now felt toward Vic. To find that he was nothing but a two-faced hypocrite just like all the rest of them.

Mitzi asked a few more questions about the trip. Roshelle gave a few more vague answers and then turned the conversation back to upcoming business. Dear, polite Mitzi, let it stay there.

Home looked better than ever. Even though she had a meeting scheduled with Newt, she went into her studio and sat down at her piano for a few minutes. She had to get her fingers back on the keys. To play a few powerful numbers. Ones she could really bang out. Songs with rhythm, with a beat, with heart. She made the place reverberate with melodies and reveled in the sense of power it gave her. She sang a few choruses and her throat felt fine, just fine. She was in great shape.

"Are you going to change before going to see Newt?" Mitzi was leaning against the door frame of the studio door. "He won't recognize you in that."

Roshelle stopped playing and looked down. She was still wearing the navy dress. It was a bit rumpled and she was tempted to throw it in the trash. "Don't worry. I'll change."

She dug in her closet for the brightest outfit she could find—the black stretch pants, cobalt blue blouse with the billowy sleeves, and her highest heels. She tied her blond hair back with a designer silk scarf and placed a bright blue, broad-brimmed hat on her head. Now she felt more like herself, she thought as she donned her sunglasses and headed out the door.

In spite of the smog, Southern California had never looked more beautiful. Carefully, she wove through the traffic on the Santa Ana Freeway toward the Valley.

The pictures of myriads of stars in Newt's outer office welcomed her back. She stood there a minute, looking around. He'd not put her picture up—yet. But he would. She'd see to that.

The front desk was empty. Sometimes Newt had a girl in as a receptionist/secretary, sometimes he didn't. Usually he ran them off with his gruffness and his penchant for working all hours of the night and day. "This business don't take no holidays," he'd say. "We don't keep no hours."

But he did keep hours—all twenty-four of them. Newt had also never been able to keep a wife. Someone told her he'd had four. He was too attached to his business to have any personal life.

His office door was ajar so she knocked, then peeked in.

He barely lifted his head from the papers in front of him. "Ah, there you are. Get yourself in here. We've got business to attend to." He waved her in and motioned her to a chair. A fat chewed cigar was stuck between two fingers.

"Just what I wanted to hear." She seated herself in a leather chair across from his cluttered desk. Newt's office was a mess, but he stayed on top of each minute detail.

He looked up from the work. "What about your sick relative back home? Everything okay?"

He was just being polite, in the brusque way that Newt had about him. He didn't require a full answer, so she simply nodded. "Everything's fine. Mitzi said you had fittings scheduled." She pulled a calendar from her purse. "You want to give those to me first."

"Man, oh man." He shuffled through the papers. "We got so much going on with you, sweets, I hardly know where to start." He pulled up a paper from under the stack. "Here, I'll just give this to you. You keep track of when you and old Louie can get together. That will be one more thing off this desk."

He sailed the fitting schedule across to her. She grabbed it and looked it over. The first session was tomorrow. She'd fill in her calendar when she got home.

"Mitzi tells me you're having second thoughts about the Camp Band. What's up? Why the switcheroo? I thought I heard in your voice you wanted to be back with those boys—wanted it in a big way."

This was the speech she'd rehearsed on the plane. She'd have to be convincing. "The sound I had with Benny," she said slowly, carefully, "and the sound I've developed since I've been singing on my own, aren't quite the same."

"Got your own style now. Is that what you're saying?"

Maybe this was going to be easier than she thought. After all, what did Newt care who she used. "That's right." She gave a little nod.

"Sorta like you outgrew his little be-bop band?" He raised one eyebrow.

She sat up. "Oh, no. I didn't mean that at all. Benny doesn't have a be-bop band. He's a great musician and a sensitive leader." She stopped short. Had he purposely trapped her?

"A great musician, huh? Sensitive, huh? But you don't want him?"

"No. I mean, it's not like that. I'd like to begin with a new group...put together a new band to back me. One that I could have fit in more with my sound. And they wouldn't already be known as a band, like Benny's is." The whole speech was falling apart. She wasn't sure if she was making any sense at all. But no way could she travel this tour with Benny Lee Camp. That's all there was to it.

Newt was still studying her face. "I see. You're the rising star now. I think if you want a new band, we can put together a little band for you. We'll need backup vocalists anyway. So we'll start scouting for the whole herd at one time."

"Will I have any say in choosing them?"

"Opinion, yes. Final say? Probably not."

She gave a little sigh. At least her opinion would count. That would do for starters. And did she want to travel by bus again? he wanted to know.

She shook her head. "Not if I can help it. I think I've paid my dues in the bus torture scene. I'd like to graduate up to flying."

"More expensive, but more expedient." He made notes as they talked.

She gave him her full attention as he began explaining the locations for the video shoots. She made notes in her calendar as he named the days they would devote to the project.

"Hopefully, if the weather cooperates, we'll have this wrapped up before the October tour begins. If not, you'll be flying back and forth to get it finished."

"No problem. I can manage that." She'd been waiting for the right time to mention her new song. Finally, he brought up the subject of the second album.

"I've written a new song, Newt. What are the chances of Mr. Laurel's letting me use it on the newest CD?"

He stopped shuffling papers and leaned back in his chair. "Good girl. You been doing some writing on your own? Old man Laurel will be glad to hear it. Is it a religious song?"

She felt herself stiffen. "Religious? Are you kidding? Of course it's not religious. What a goofy thing to ask me."

"It ain't goofy. Ted Laurel wants you to have one religious number on your next CD. Says you got a bit of a reputation for singing one at the clubs and it's sorta become a trademark of your show. Know what I mean? After all, even Elvis sang religious songs."

A trademark? She couldn't believe this. "I can't. I won't. He can't make me, can he? It's not in the contract or anything." Now she really wished Benny would have looked over that contract before she signed it.

"Of course it's not in the contract. But we didn't figure you'd have a conniption. You sung 'em all over the country for every joint between here and Tuscaloosa." He waved the chewed cigar at her. "How was we to know you'd get bent all out of shape about putting one little religious song on a CD?"

"This is different."

"Women," he muttered. "Never can figure 'em out."

"This is one time I put my foot down. Absolutely no religious songs on my CDs." Her promise to Grandma Riley was for ending performances only. That was all she had promised. She never promised to put one on every record she cut. Her trademark indeed! She'd have to put a stop to that notion immediately. She'd rather be an out and out rank sinner than to be a hypocrite, having people think she was something she wasn't.

"So what about my song?" she asked again. "What are my chances?"

"I'll feel him out and let you know what he says." He ran his fingers through his graying hair. "Only now I'll have to figure out whether to tell him about the new song before or after I tell him you refuse to sing one itsy bitsy little religious number."

But she knew Newt was a manipulator and a negotiator. He sounded miffed, but he was in her corner. If anyone could pave the way with Ted Laurel, Newt could do it.

twelve

Rodeo Drive smelled of money. The Beverly Hills Hotel rose to a majestic height and commanded acres of space at Rodeo Drive and Sunset Boulevard. The unmistakable green and pink stucco surrounded by giant palms and lush colorful foliage, spoke of elegance and exclusivity.

As Roshelle drove by, she tried to imagine the hundreds of famous faces that had entered there through the years. She had often told herself she cared nothing about all the trappings of fame, that her only passion was to sing. But now she realized the money was nice, very nice. It felt great to be able to buy the things she'd always wanted.

The name SARVIANO ORIGINALS was scrolled in bright red letters across the front of Louis's studio. Roshelle found a parking place nearby and hurried up the front steps for her early morning appointment. As she understood it, Louis had already met with the producers of the music video and costumes had been discussed. Her input was needed.

Now that Roshelle and Louis had been working together for a while, Mitzi was no longer asked to come along as a chaperon. She breezed through the shop and into the back as though she'd been doing this forever. It seemed so right, so natural.

"Hello, gorgeous," Louis called to her as he emerged from a group of bustling workers and racks of dresses. "How's my favorite up-and-coming singer?" He reached for her hand and pecked a kiss on it. "You're looking wonderful as usual."

Roshelle was trying to learn to keep all the gushing industry remarks in perspective, but it sounded so soothing to her ears. "Thanks, Louis. Am I late?"

He released her hand gently. "Perfect timing." His laughing eyes danced and the dimples appeared. "But I wouldn't mind waiting for one as lovely as you."

He had a way of making her blush and when he noticed, his eyes were all the merrier. "What's first on the agenda?" she asked.

"This way." He placed his hand on her waist to guide her back to his office. There they looked over sketches and fabric swatches. He explained what the producers has suggested for each cut on the CD, then he asked her pointed questions. On a yellow legal pad, he took down her comments as she voiced her thoughts and opinions.

Several dresses for the concert tour were ready and each needed a fitting. Little work was needed, however because he now knew her size and her tastes. Each dress was spectacular but when he brought out the jade green with the flared mermaid skirt filled with ruffles, she gasped with delight.

"This is wonderful. Too, too wonderful." She ran her hand over the glossy material, which was almost iridescent as it shimmered in the light.

He smiled. "I thought you might like this." He put it up to her. "Perfect with your light skin. When I saw this fabric I knew immediately that I wanted to do something a little special for you."

"A little special? This is more than a little special."

She hurried to the dressing room to slip into it. It fit

perfectly. This dress would be a show-stopper for sure. Outside, Louis helped her up onto the small platform before the mirrors where he could check out every seam. She felt as though her heart were absolutely going to burst. She danced across the platform and laughed as she went. She was floating on a euphoric cloud.

Louis sat back and watched, laughing with her. "It moves well, right?"

She twirled a couple of times and let the ruffled, flared skirt fly. "Perfectly." She looked down at him. "You are truly a genius."

"Even a genius needs something to work with, love. And you are a beautiful creation for me to clothe in my beautiful creations."

The fittings took all morning. As they were finishing up, Louis casually asked if she would have lunch with him.

His invitation was a surprise. She was brushing her hair in front of one of the many mirrors and she brushed back the soft bangs and watched as they fell back on her forehead. "I didn't know busy people like you stopped for lunch," she said.

"You can bet it takes something—or someone—quite exceptional to cause me to stop."

His eyes were always laughing so it was difficult to tell if he meant it, or if he were just going on. But then, what if he were just going on? So what? She had no one to go to lunch with, and it might be fun. Work couldn't always consume her.

The restaurant he chose was just down the street and they walked the distance together. He tucked her arm in his as they strolled together. "I've been listening to all

your songs on the CD and I think they're superb," he said
waving his free hand to emphasize the point. "I can see
why Ted Laurel is so elated these days. I've not seen him
this bubbly in months. You have a natural talent. . .," he
paused as he searched for the word, "refreshing, I guess
one could say. We hear so much of the other, you know,
mediocre singers who are pushed into the spotlight. You
seem to be soaring."

Was this true? Was she different? Did she possess a
natural talent that could take her to the top? She loved to
hear him say it, but was it true? And how could she know?

They chose to sit in the garden amidst the orange and
lemon trees beneath the pink-and-white striped umbrellas.
She scanned the menu and marveled. Most of the things
listed, she'd never tasted so she deferred the ordering
duties to Louis. His favorite, he explained, was escargots
baked in baby russet potatoes with hot garlic butter. She
flinched, but found it was indeed delicious. She would
even learn how to eat like a star.

Louis was a jovial companion and he kept her laughing
throughout lunch. His lighthearted and nonsensical bantering was in stark contrast to the heaviness she'd encoun-
tered in Tulsa.

He was careful to watch the time, though, and didn't let
lunch take her afternoon or his. As he walked her back to
where her car was parked, he thanked her with a light kiss
on the cheek. "Do you like the beach?" he wanted to know,
as he opened the car door for her.

She nodded. "I love the beach."

"How about a Sunday afternoon at the beach? Will you
go with me?"

The invitation was tempting—just what she needed—

but she remembered the hectic schedule facing her. "I have no idea what's coming up—what all Newt has planned. When the shooting begins, he says we work straight though until it's done."

"And your tour begins soon after, right?" He wet the tip of his finger with his tongue and pretended to be writing on his palm. "Let's see, make a note to fit in time to have one short fling with Louis Sarviano."

She laughed. "I'm sure I'll have a few free moments somewhere, I'm just not sure where. I'll know more next week. Perhaps by the next fitting session." She slipped into her car and looked up at him. A lock of the curly dark hair had carelessly fallen on his forehead. She found herself comparing his face to Vic's, then quickly shut out the thought.

He reached in the car window to take her hand. "Let's shake on that. One of those free moments belongs to me." He squeezed her hand then let her go. His laughing smile was etched in her brain as she drove home.

Louis was a highly successful man in the industry, in fact top of the line in his business. He'd probably met hundreds of stars and yet he wanted to be with her. She was amazed.

With joy and exuberance, Roshelle threw herself into the filming sessions. Up early, into bed late, she loved every waking second of the work. The drama of acting out the parts fascinated her. Other singers had advanced from singing into acting, perhaps it would happen with her as well.

These were the thoughts that ran through her mind while she was on location, lip-synching her own songs, as the tapes were rolling. One location was on the craggy rocks above the pounding surf near Santa Barbara. The rugged beauty of the area was magnificent. The wind wildly blew her hair, but it was just the effect the producers wanted.

Roshelle made up her mind she would ask around about acting school. She wanted to know more and more about this business of acting, as well as music. She already knew how to put herself into the mood and message of a song and probably it wouldn't be much different to put herself into a character and act out a part. She savored the delicious thought. There was so much to this magical kingdom—and she wanted more!

Phone calls and cards had come from Victor Moran. She sent the cards back and failed to return the calls. Hopefully, their paths would never cross again. Seldom did she think about Dr. Beasley's words spoken to her that day in Tulsa and his warning went unheeded. She worked hard to forget everything that had happened in Tulsa. Only late at night, when she had trouble sleeping, did she feel the fear creep back in. The pain pills helped some but the discomfort in her throat never went away completely. Staying busy was the answer; sometimes using sleeping pills was part of the answer as well.

One sunny Sunday, she called Louis to let him know she had the day free. She hesitated at first to call, wondering if he'd been serious, but his infectious laughter and quick acceptance extinguished her doubts.

They took the Pacific Coast Freeway to Laguna Beach where their lunch was served on a brick-tiled patio over-looking the azure Pacific. The restaurant patio was furnished with white tables and chairs, each chair padded with a bright blue cushion. White grilled ironwork fences enclosed the eating area, with pots of red geraniums perched on each support post. Down from the restaurant, Roshelle could see hundreds of sun worshippers enjoying the sandy beach and the magnificent waves. The lazy atmosphere relaxed her right down to her bones.

"You look even more lovely with that half smile on your lips," Louis said as he sipped his wine. "Tell me what you're thinking."

"To be truthful, I wasn't thinking. I feel so rested here, it seems like work just to think."

He laughed. "You have been working hard, Roshelle. You need to take time for yourself. Like me. I give myself several play days each month."

"Play days?" She stirred a glass of iced mocha, having chosen to forego the liquor.

"Days in which I do nothing but play all day. Deep sea fishing, snorkeling, scuba diving, swimming, tennis, you name it."

"Your play sounds as hard as your work," she retorted. Louis exuded a sense of vitality and kinetic energy. He made her feel excited just being around him.

He cocked his head as if to think about her remark. "I suppose you're right. I don't do anything halfway. I work hard and play hard."

After they had finished off their cold plates consisting of cheeses, melons, boiled eggs, and slaw, Louis took her hand to walk down to the beach. He told her funny stories of the stars with whom he had worked. And stories of how he started his business as a boy in high school.

"Think about it," he said, as they spread their bright towels on the warm sand, "a boy who thinks about, talks about, and sketches women's dresses isn't going to be all that popular, right? Right. And my little Italian mama wanted me to open a restaurant like my Uncle Primo. My big old papa, he just says, 'Please boy, do *anything* but draw pictures of ladies nighties.'" He laughed at his own pantomime to describe his father and she laughed with him. She doffed her white eyelet coverup, and he gave a whistle. "Love that swimsuit, Rosh. Looks great on you."

She flopped down on her stomach on her towel. He pulled the bottle of tanning lotion from her bag, poured an ample handful, and proceeded to apply it to her back in gentle circular motions. "I didn't have too much support for my singing when I was a kid, either," she told him.

"You don't say," he said as he continued to apply the lotion down her shoulders and arms. "As beautiful as you sing, I would think your family would have been very proud."

"As long as I sang what they wanted me to sing, I was okay."

"And what was that?"

"Church music."

He gave a little grunt of understanding. "Ah, and that's all? Nothing else? No other kinds of music."

"You got it."

"What a pity." He gave her a little shake. "Come on, Miss Ramone, you need to learn how to float the waves."

"But I was just getting comfortable," she protested, not wanting to move. She had sunk comfortably into the depression of the soft sand and felt she could sleep the afternoon away.

"But the waves are calling." He then flopped her over and before she knew what was happening, she was bundled up in his muscular arms and he was headed to the water.

At first she fought and protested, then she laughed and giggled. He carried her right into the warm foamy waves. "Hold your breath," he warned as he plunged them both into the ocean water. She screamed with delight.

They spent the afternoon playing in the waves. He taught her how to ride the waves in and commended her for her quick learning. She told him about learning to swim in Grandma Riley's pond and how adept she became at diving off the old wooden dock. "I should have been born by the ocean," she said as they ran dripping to the towels. "I feel cheated." She sat down and pushed her hair back out of her eyes.

"But now you have the happy California sun and surf at your doorstep to make up for it," he said. He wrapped an extra towel around her shoulders and as he did, he easily pushed her back on the sand and leaned across her and began to kiss her. "And you have Louis to make up for another lack in your life, too," he whispered to her between the kisses.

At first the fiery kisses were exciting to her, but as they became more demanding and intimate, she tried to push him off. "Please, Louis," she protested. "This is too soon. Too fast."

He stopped kissing her, but his face was close to hers, his blue eyes still dancing. "Fast is how things are done here," he said softly. "And I'm not used to any woman saying 'stop' to me."

"This one is saying 'stop.' Please."

Reluctantly, he loosened his hold, but kept his arm around her. "Sort of an old-fashioned girl, aren't you?" he said with a touch of amazement.

It was odd to hear him say that. She wanted to think she

was as contemporary as all the others in this business but maybe she wasn't. If Benny were here, he'd take this guy to the laundry and hang him out to dry.

He lightly kissed her nose. "All right then, I'll take things a little slower from now on," he said.

The incident put only a small damper on the rest of the day. In spite of the scare, Roshelle was still glad she went with him. Learning to float the waves had been worth it.

Yet another appearance in Vegas was squeezed in, for which she was thankful. She needed to be sure, before the tour, that she still had the punch it took to deliver the goods to a live audience. The response left no doubt in her mind. Due to the album, the crowds were bigger than ever. Newt also wanted a chance for her to work with the new band and the backup singers. He even flew to Vegas to catch one of the shows so he could see for himself. He gave them all a "thumbs up."

"Guess you were right about needing a new sound," he told her after the show. "This band is terrific."

She chafed at his comments, feeling guilty for having cut Benny out. She'd not talked to him for weeks and she avoided asking Newt about the Camp Band at all. It was less painful that way.

The first week in October, she flew to Cleveland for the first leg of the tour; Mitzi was by her side. The tour was vastly different than traveling by bus to noisy clubs where few people listened. These were concerts where the people purchased tickets, just to come and hear her sing. She often thought of that mockingbird on the tiny tip-top limb. She was shaky at times, but she would sing her heart out.

Each night she was in a different city. Toledo, Detroit, Columbus, Pittsburgh—the cities all began to bleed together after a while. The spotlights, the applause, the heady music, the well-wishers, the autograph seekers—it was infectious and intoxicating.

By the end of the second week, Roshelle was beginning to feel the effects of the strain. She was backstage after the show in Minneapolis when she realized she was out of pain medication. She'd been in touch with Dr. Beasley only to refill the prescription; eventually, she'd have to see a physician in L.A. in order to get the prescription there.

She had gone to great lengths to hide the pills and the phone calls, from Mitzi. Dear Mitzi, who knew more about her business than she did. Why hadn't she kept closer watch on the pills? She was angry at herself and her nerves felt jumpy. She was starting to slip out of her finale dress when suddenly there was a knock at the dressing room door. Mitzi ran to get it.

"It's security," she called back over her shoulder to Roshelle. "You know anyone by the name of Ingram?"

"You know all the people I know," she snapped back. "You tell me."

"Ingram, Ingram," Mitzi said, then shook her head. "Sorry, Miss Ramone doesn't know anyone by that name." She closed the door.

In a moment there was another knock. Roshelle could hear the voice of the security man again. "This Ingram dame says she's a sister to Miss Ramone."

Roshelle jumped up from where she was sitting. "It's Janey!"

thirteen

There was a tumble of laughter and introductions as Janey was let in with the sleeping Darla slung over her shoulder like a sack of flour. The other shoulder was weighted down with a diaper bag.

"Did you jostle through that crowd with the baby? Your arms must be killing you. Here, lay her down on the settee. What are you doing in Minneapolis? Are you alone?" The questions spilled out of Roshelle, as she felt new bubbly joy rising up inside her. Her own little sister, right here in Minneapolis.

Carefully, Janey unloaded the precious bundle. Almost before the baby was down, Mitzi was kneeling down by the settee. "She's beautiful," she said as she touched the cheek, red from where it had lain against Janey's shoulder. "Isn't she beautiful, Rosh? Your own little niece." She looked up from where she sat on the floor. "I want to have at least four."

Rosh was surprised. "Four babies?"

"Sure. Why not?"

Mitzi had never spoken of her own future plans in life. She was so intertwined into Roshelle's business, the subject never came up.

"We're here visiting Alex's parents when we saw in the paper about your concert," Janey explained. "I had to come and see. You're wonderful! Just wonderful! And all those people love you."

"You *paid* for tickets?"

"Of course. How else do you get in?"

"Silly girl, if you'd called I would have given you tickets."

"It was hard enough just getting back here," Janey said with a little laugh. "Besides, Mom explained that it was almost impossible to get hold of you, so I didn't even bother."

Roshelle felt a twinge of uneasiness. In keeping distanced from her mother and Uncle Jess, she'd inadvertently cut Janey off as well. But she never meant to. "I'm so sorry I didn't call you back when I was in Tulsa in August," Roshelle began to explain.

Janey waved away the apology. "Hey, I knew you were busy. It was Mother who insisted I have the little dinner."

"Mother? But she said—"

The rousing Darla interrupted her. The tiny face screwed up into the beginnings of a cry. "She'll be ready for a bottle," Janey said, digging in the bag.

"Oh, can I?" Mitzi asked. "How about if I take Darla into one of the other dressing rooms so the two of you can talk a while."

"Better than that, can you come over to the hotel and stay for the night?" Roshelle asked.

Janey shook her head. "Alex is waiting. We have to get back to his folks' place. We agreed that I'd come back and let you see Darla for a few minutes. I wasn't even sure I could get in."

"I'm sorry," Roshelle apologized again, thinking of her little sister struggling to get in to see her. If she were in her shoes, Roshelle wasn't sure she'd have bothered.

Roshelle watched as Mitzi eagerly took baby and bottle

off by herself. "I can do this. I had scads of younger siblings. I was raised as a babysitter," she said proudly as she marched out the door.

"Janey, I did plan to call you that night. Something came up."

"For such a versatile singer, you sure are hung up on one note. Is that the only song you can sing?" Janey gave her sister a hug. "Forget all that. Let's talk about this dress. I can't believe how beautiful you look." She put her hands on Roshelle's shoulders and turned her around slowly. "Is this made just for you? I mean, you don't pick these things off a rack somewhere, right?"

"It's made exclusively for me. I have a wardrobe stylist who works with me."

Janey mouthed the words "wardrobe stylist" without speaking, then rolled her eyes. "And all the band and the singers. Do you travel with all of them?"

"All over the country."

"I'm so proud of you. I have your CD and play it constantly. I love to think back and remember how you used to sit at the piano and sing for hours. I knew you would be great. I've told Alex all about you. He's proud of me for having a sister like you."

Janey's open adoration was making her uncomfortable. She steered Janey toward the settee and motioned for her to sit down. "How's Uncle Jess?" she asked to change the subject. She stepped behind the screen to slip out of the dress and into her satin robe. Sitting at the dressing table, she began dipping into the makeup remover and smearing it on her face.

"He's better. He rallied soon after your visit and went home the next week. He still uses a walker, but he's stronger every day."

"But Mother made it seem. . . ." She didn't finish.

"He was dangerously ill. She was right about that. The first reports weren't good at all. We were all pretty frightened."

"Okay, that was genuine. What about her telling me that you cried all evening because I didn't come out to Sandott to see you?"

Janey smiled. "That was one of her exaggerations. If I'd known, I'd have told you there was no pressure on you to come. I didn't realize what she was doing."

Roshelle marveled at her sister's serenity. "What you call an exaggeration, I call a lie. How can you stand to live near her?" She knew the answer to that question before she spoke it. After all, Janey always got along with everyone.

"It's not always easy," Janey admitted. "But you know how hurt and wounded she is. You probably know much better than I do."

Hurt and wounded? Cora Rayford? Hurting and wounding *others* was closer to the truth.

"She's harder on herself than anyone," Janey went on. "She blames herself for so many things gone wrong. The guilt's beginning to take its toll."

"You'll excuse me if I don't get out my crying towel," Roshelle remarked, grabbing for a tissue and waving it.

"Everyone makes mistakes," Janey countered. "She did what she thought was right."

"Please, spare me." Roshelle swiped at the remover, whisking off the heavy stage makeup. "She's as hard as nails. What she 'thought was right' nearly drove me to suicide. She and Uncle Jess are both the type who know how everyone *else* should live. They're miserable, so they set out to make life miserable for everyone else."

Janey rose and stepped over to the makeup mirror. "It's not an unsolvable problem." She gave a little laugh. "Mother detested Alex when I first met him and she tried every way in the world to scare him off. But we hung in there. Now she brags about her intelligent son-in-law. Alex and I are praying for the Lord to heal her wounds and change her life. To bring her joy back again."

Roshelle gave a snort. "Again? What makes you think she ever had any." She glanced up in the mirror at Janey standing behind her. She regretted the words as soon as she saw the look on Janey's face. She whirled around. "Hey Janey, I'm sorry. I love you, Sis, but please don't come in her harping about Mother. Frankly I don't *care* if she changes from the mean witch into the kind witch. I work hard each day to not even think about her *or* Uncle Jess. Their ideas of religion makes me ill."

Janey gave a little sigh. "I know sometimes they don't do a very good job of it." Then she smiled. "But that's what I love about Jesus so much. He doesn't let us into heaven on the basis of how other people live out their faith."

Roshelle was relieved that Mitzi and the baby came back in at that moment. Mitzi held up the empty bottle like a banner. "She took every drop."

"Thanks so much," Janey said. "I never expected a ready-made babysitter backstage."

"This was a pleasure. What a little doll," Mitzi said, planting mushy kisses all over the baby's face. "She's so good. All the noise in this crazy place, and it doesn't faze her."

"You don't have to tell me," Janey said, chuckling. "I'm

already convinced."

"Rosh, you have a darling niece," she said to Roshelle who was now changed and in her street makeup. "Here, hold her a minute. I didn't mean to hog her."

Darla was cooing and chewing on her fist. Roshelle breathed in the good aromas of baby as she took her into her arms. "She looks like you," Roshelle told Janey.

"That's what everyone says." The pride was evident in her voice.

Roshelle caressed the baby's hair with her lips. She had almost forgotten the exquisite downy softness of a baby's hair and skin. "Mmm, you smell so good and feel so soft." And Darla replied with a little gurgle that sounded almost like a laugh.

"I must get out to where Alex is waiting," Janey told them. "He's a sweet, patient guy, but I'm not sure he's *this* patient."

Reluctantly, Roshelle handed the baby back. There's something about a baby, she thought, that speaks of peace and quiet trust.

There were hugs, a few tears, and sweet goodbyes. Roshelle gave Newt's office number to Janey and said, "He always knows where I am. If you need me, call him."

"I will, Rosh," Janey said with a catch in her voice.

The momentum of the tour continued to build and reviews were strong and positive. There were big cities and midsize cities; there were large civic centers and smaller theaters; there were lavish dressing rooms and more decrepit dressing rooms; there were receptive audiences and then there were wild audiences. For the most part, she was received with open arms. She gave phone interviews, backstage interviews, and even a couple of hotel lobby interviews. Almost overnight, it seemed that the whole world wanted to see and talk to Roshelle Ramone.

As the mild fall weather turned sharply cooler, the tour advanced southward. For this, Roshelle was thankful to Newt. He now knew how much she detested cold weather.

Suddenly one night they were in Miami, and she remembered back to the time they played the nightclub in the beach-front hotel. That was the night Benny got so bent out of shape because of Vic. Poor Benny. And Keel met her out on the beach and, in his left-handed sort of way, tried to talk her into marrying Benny.

She thought of Benny and the band and wondered where they were and how they were doing. She supposed a girl could do a lot worse than marry someone like Benny. He was steady, reliable, and fiercely loyal. Her conscience pricked her now whenever she thought of how she avoided calling him before the tour and she had to continually remind herself why she hadn't. But the guilt never lessened.

And it was in Miami where she first met Victor. It occurred to her that he might try to see her again here in Miami; it seemed like something Victor Moran might do. She had an idea he probably tracked the route of her tour. He had finally stopped trying to call her and the lavender cards had stopped coming as well. That was a relief. At least she thought it was a relief. Sometimes, as she directed Mitzi to return one, she found herself wondering what he might have written inside.

But, thankfully, Vic wasn't in Miami and after the Miami stint, Newt had scheduled a few days' break. Heaving big sighs of relief, she and Mitzi caught a plane for L.A.

"I think I'll sleep for days," Roshelle said as the plane touched down in beautiful Southern California.

"I think I'll grill a chicken and eat the whole thing." Mitzi seemed to hate restaurant food worse than any other part of the tour. Not that she was a big eater, just the opposite. She was a picky eater and enjoyed her own cooking more than any other. In the few short months since they'd had their own place, she was constantly throwing together superb dishes.

Roshelle was always surprised at how "homey" Mitzi was. And yet she braved the traumas of travel like a trouper. She needed to do something special for her friend to say thank you. Now that there were a few free days, perhaps there would be time to shop for a nice gift for Mitzi. But, before she could purchase one, she, herself, became the recipient of a gift.

The evening they arrived home, Louis Sarviano came to visit. She and Mitzi were in the living room with their feet up, going on and on about how good it was to be home. In spite of her protests, he insisted she change and go with him to supper. Roshelle knew what that meant—dress *up*.

Mitzi seemed amused at the whole thing. "Want me to help you pick out your outfit? Or stay here and entertain your guest?" she asked with a smile.

"Help me pick out an outfit, *then* come back and entertain my guest."

Mitzi giggled as she loped up the stairs, two at a time.

They decided on the silk, double-breasted, pale pink coat that went best with her pearls. Dressy, but still comfortable.

Louis took her to one of the "seen and be seen" spots in

Beverly Hills and she was not sorry she had accepted his invitation. In fact, as soon as she was seated in his Porshe coupe, he began his light, funny bantering and she realized she had actually missed him.

The evening was beautiful and the maitre d' quickly knew that Mr. Sarviano wanted a table for two on the restaurant terrace. Ever since the day at the beach, he'd been every inch a gentleman, as though he wanted to respect her wishes.

Following dinner, he took her on a drive to the beach. There, on a spot overlooking the moonlit water, he presented her with a diamond bracelet.

"It's just a little thing," he said, almost apologetically, "but somehow I wanted to give you a token of how much I care about you."

Roshelle was stunned. This was so sudden. She looked at this wildly handsome man with the dimples, flashing smile, and dark curls. Any woman in her right mind would be thrilled to be seen with him, let alone receive his attention in this way.

Before she could speak, he had the bracelet out of the box and was fastening it on her wrist. It fit perfectly.

"Your wrist is so tiny," he said, kissing her hand softly. "I knew to get a small size."

"Thank you, Louis. It's so beautiful. I don't know what to say."

He put his fingers to her lips. "You don't have to say anything right now. Just give me a chance."

"A chance?"

"A chance to get to know you, for you to know me. A chance to build a relationship."

"That's going to be difficult with the schedules we

keep." She wasn't even sure she wanted to give him a chance. Her mind was spinning.

"Difficult, maybe. Impossible? Never."

She looked at the bracelet on her arm, sparkling even in the dim light of the moon. "I can't keep this, Louis—"

"Nonsense. This is a gift to show you I care. It has no strings attached." He lifted his hands up in surrender. "What do I have to say?" His eyes danced as he laughed. "You've done a number on me, Roshelle. And I didn't even realize it until you were gone all those weeks." He reached out to take her hand again, touching the bracelet. "I'm falling in love with you, Roshelle. If I hadn't thought I'd scare you completely away, it would have been a ring rather than a bracelet." Then he kissed her. Not with the violence she had experienced on the beach, but gently and sweetly.

The next day, when Mitzi saw the bracelet and heard the news, she was ecstatic. "Rosh, you've blown this guy away. All these dames he's been working with for years, but you walk in and knock him cold in one swoop. Way to go!"

"But, Mitzi, I'm not in love with this guy. He wants to build a serious relationship and I want to build a career."

Mitzi gave a flip of her hand. "Get to know him, marry his money, and sing for a hobby."

"You're no help." She perched on a kitchen bar stool and watched as Mitzi whipped up a soufflé for their breakfast.

"I'm kidding, silly." She whipped the eggs with a vengeance. "Just because a guy likes you, or even falls in love with you, is no reason you have to *do* anything. Just let it ride and see what happens. In fact, the next time he asks you out you could say 'No, read my lips, spelled N-O!' "

Roshelle took a swallow of hot coffee. "Of course, you're right." She laughed. "I hadn't thought of that."

A phone call from Newt interrupted their conversation. "Hey, sweets! Got a meeting lined up for you this afternoon. A recording company interested in you cutting a CD for them."

"But Newt, I'm signed with Laurel."

"Only for two. Life will go on after the second album, you know. I've worked with this guy some before. He knows his business. This afternoon at three. Okay?"

"I'll be there."

She hung up as Mitzi pushed the steamy soufflé in front of her. She stabbed at it with her fork. "And I said I was going to rest for these few days."

"No rest for the wicked," quipped Mitzi as she touched the gleaming bracelet dangling on Roshelle's arm.

Roshelle rolled up the sleeves on the long, loose-fitting jacket she had pulled on over her gabardine slacks and her checkered shirt.

As she headed for the front door, Mitzi called out to her. "Wait a minute. Where are you going in that getup?"

"To Newt's office."

"I thought you said he had a guy interested in working with you."

"He does."

Mitzi stood leaning against the door frame with her arms folded, shaking her head.

Roshelle looked down at her outfit. "Not right, huh?"

"Not unless you're applying for housekeeper."

Roshelle sighed. "Must be a backlash. Never thought I'd tire of pretty dresses and spike heels."

Mitzi walked over and put her arm around Roshelle's shoulder. "Come on. Maybe Mama Mitzi can help little Roshie find a compromise."

Later, when Roshelle stepped out of her car in the parking lot at Newt's office she felt much more sure of herself dressed in the navy-and-rose, floral-print dress with a sweeping skirt. Mitzi helped her fix a lacy rose ribbon that caught her hair at the nape of her neck. With a bit of new excitement, she strolled into the familiar cluttered office.

There was now a young girl at the desk, which meant Newt was trying out another one. Before the girl could even announce Roshelle's arrival, he was hollering at her to come on in.

She walked through the door to see Vic sitting there, smiling at her.

fourteen

"Hey, sweets, you're looking great." Newt came from around his desk to give her a hug. "Come on in here. I want you to meet an old business friend of mine, Victor Moran." He led her to the leather chair beside Vic and seated her there.

Her body was tense. She'd been put on the defensive and she didn't like it. What right did he have to come here like this? "Your 'old business friend' and I have met," she said, not bothering to keep the ice from her voice.

"That right?" Newt was back around the opposite side of the cluttered desk. He sunk into his squeaky chair. "Mr. Moran never told me that."

"Mr. Hardcastle never asked," Vic said in that quiet even way of his.

Roshelle had never seen Newt ruffled, but now he seemed to be stifling a grin. It made her even more irritated. "What's going on here?" she demanded.

Newt, obviously sensing her irritation, shrugged to show his innocence in the matter. "This is a business meeting, sweets, pure and simple. Mr. Moran here called and asked if we could talk about your cutting a CD for his company."

"But his company puts out religious music."

"I told him you wouldn't be too keen on the notion," Newt said. "If you won't do it for Ted Laurel, I was sure you wouldn't do it for no stranger. That's what I told him."

He punctuated the remarks with the chewed cigar and leaned back in the chair. " Course that was when I didn't know he wasn't no stranger."

"You told him exactly right," she said, not looking at Vic.

"Hey now, slow down," Newt said. "The guy's come all this way. Why not let's give him a chance to speak his piece."

"Let's do," Vic agreed.

Roshelle allowed her silence to indicate her reluctant agreement.

"I've come to offer you a contract to cut a CD for the Moran label of all inspirational songs." Vic drew a paper from his pocket. "I have all the paperwork right here."

"I looked at it," Newt put in. "It ain't bad."

She took a breath to speak, but Vic jumped back in. "There are so many hurting people out there, Roshelle," his quiet voice went on. "I saw how your voice and your style can touch listeners. That night in Vegas, you were able to touch them in the midst of all the clamor and hoopla. They were deeply moved." He paused a moment. "But I not only heard it, I felt it, too. An album like this could help so many people."

"Aw, come on, sweets. What's a few religious songs? Even Elvis—"

"I know, I know. Even Elvis Presley sang religious songs. The answer is no."

"But you been singing one a night for years," Newt protested. "It don't make no sense."

"I won't be a hypocrite." Now she looked at Vic. "I told you the very first time I met you why I sing a hymn after every performance. I promised my Grandma Riley before she died that I would. But I didn't make her any promises about records. The more I do this, the more people will think I'm some kind of religious spokesperson, and I'm not. I don't want to be known like that. And you're tempting me to even give up singing hymns in live concerts. It's already causing misunderstandings!"

She stood as she turned to Newt. "And you should have known better than to have even considered it. The next time please check with me first, or I'll. . .I'll be looking for a new agent." She shut the door hard as she walked out.

"The nerve of some people," she muttered as the receptionist stared at her.

She fussed and fumed all the way back to the house. She was sorry she ever called Vic when she was in Tulsa. Sorry she ever went out with him. And sorry she ever let him kiss her. She wished she'd never told him anything about herself. "Me? Helping hurting people? What a laugh."

As soon as she stepped in the front door, Mitzi was calling to her. "Newt wants you to call right away. What happened when you were there? The old toughie seems almost beside himself."

She threw down her tote bag on the couch and dialed the number. She was even angrier at Vic for making her upset at her own agent.

"Look," he said as his voice came on the line, "I'm really sorry, sweets. He never told me you two knew each other. And I never knew none of this stuff about your old dying granny. You oughta tell me these things. I can't read your mind, you know."

She was sorry she'd blown up at Newt. It certainly wasn't his fault. "I'm sorry, too, Newt. Sorry I let that guy get me rankled at you. But you have to watch his kind. They can be really sneaky."

"Right. I ain't used to working with no religious folk. In fact, I worked with Moran before he got religion."

"Really?"

"Yeah, when his old man was still bankrolling him."

"Why did he stop? The father, I mean."

"The way I heard it, when Moran got religion—it was in all the papers—his whole family disowned him. Pushed him right out of the nest and took away the gravy train. One day he was a millionaire playboy with a few Miami nightspots as his toys, the next day, a penniless nobody."

Roshelle tried to assimilate this information into the midst of the anger she was feeling. After all, what did she care what kind of family he came from or what kind of treatment he'd received?

Newt didn't stop to catch his breath before he jumped into the next subject. "But I called to tell you terrific good news. This'll make you forget this afternoon ever happened." He let a meaningful moment of silence lapse to emphasize the build up. "You ready for this? I got you on the Freddie Fremont talk show."

She let out a squeal. "Oh, Newt, you're great. When?" Fremont's late night show was a prime-time spot.

Mitzi was standing nearby with a questioning look. Roshelle mouthed, "Freddie Fremont show," and Mitzi gave a whoop.

"The week after the tour is finished. Perfect timing, if you ask me," Newt was saying.

"Perfect," she agreed.

Before hanging up, Newt asked, "Say, just for the record, what did the religious dude mean about that night in Vegas? I mean, he must have felt or seen something."

"Newt, my friend, I have no earthly idea. Must have been his over-active imagination."

But, as she hung up the phone, she knew that was a lie. Vic was talking about the moving of the Holy Spirit. She'd felt it many times as a girl, before Daddy died. And she'd felt it that night in Vegas.

Roshelle made sure before they went on the road again, that she was well-stocked with her pain medication— along with the blessed sleeping pills.

The last part of the tour was a swing through the south, and it was almost better than the first. Now she felt more like a veteran; now she knew the ropes. Both she and Mitzi were learning how to cope with the demands of the grueling pace.

Two weeks before Thanksgiving, the tour came to a close. Their last night was a whiz-bang show in New Orleans and Roshelle was ecstatic. As Newt had said, it was the perfect time to be on Freddie's show.

She was more nervous backstage at the television studio than she'd been at her own concerts. She studied her dress in the full-length mirrors. The black velvet, fitted bodice had a sweetheart neckline, puffed sleeves, and a touch of golden lace at the dropped waist. The full skirt of gold-dotted black taffeta shimmered and swished as she gently turned about.

Suddenly, she was terrified—she was a singer not a speaker. Even though she'd gone over things with Newt and the public relations people, she still felt uneasy.

Her biggest fear was that he'd ask her about singing the hymns and so she came up with several rational answers to give him. But she needn't have bothered because the subject was never touched. Only later did she realize that people like Freddie cared little about such matters.

Her entry song was received with enthusiastic applause by the live studio audience. That was the best part of the show.

When she was seated, Freddie asked various general questions about her exploding career. They talked about the tour and its success and the album and its success. The name of the album was mentioned several times, as was the title of her hit song. These are the things Newt said were important.

"Your fans gotta know what to go buy," he had told her during the briefing.

Just when the interview seemed wrapped up and she was happy about every part of it, Freddie said, "And now I understand there are wedding bells ringing in your life."

Nothing he could have said would have shocked her more. Her mind went blank. This had not been rehearsed. It hadn't even been discussed. "You must have the wrong woman," she said when her composure was regained. "Marriage is low on my 'things to do' list."

"Aw now, come on. You don't need to be shy with us. Everyone knows you and Beverly Hills's most eminent dress designer, Louis Sarviano, are a hot number these days."

Louis? How could anyone know of us, she thought to herself.

"How handy to have your own designer as your mate. Seems to go together rather nicely, I think," Freddie went on. "Did he design this little number you have on?" He waved his hand toward her black dress.

"No," she answered quickly. "He didn't." How could she clear this up before it went any farther?

"But he has designed many of your stage costumes, right?"

She nodded. "Louis is a genius when it comes to dress designs, but—"

"And he had something to do with this little number, too, right?" He reached out to where her arm was leaning on his desk, and touched the diamond bracelet.

Roshelle thrashed about in her mind for something to say, while striving to maintain her stage smile. "The bracelet was a gift from Louis, but it's not what you think."

"What *I* think?" Freddie turned to the audience. "Just look at this hunk of ice," he said as the nearest camera zoomed in on her wrist. "And she wants us to think this isn't serious." He got the ripple of laughter he sought and appeared pleased.

And Newt had told her that Freddie was a friendly interviewer, she thought.

He obviously sensed her discomfort and was going for more. "We'll try to get the famous Mr. Sarviano on here in a few weeks to tell his side of this story. What to do you think?" The audience cheered and applauded. He turned back to Roshelle with a sardonic smile. "Personally, I think the two of you would make a striking twosome." Again he fished for audience response, and again they applauded their full agreement.

"Much as I'd like to play along with this little game," she said with more force than before, "I'll have to tell you that I have no intention of marrying Mr. Sarviano. We're friends and friends only."

"But he has asked, we understand." Freddie was

relentless.

"No," she could say quite honestly. "He has never asked. There's no place in my life for marriage at this time."

It seemed like an eternity before he finally said, "We'll be right back after this announcement."

Due to the live audience, Roshelle had no opportunity to say to Freddie what she was thinking and she was quickly escorted off.

Mitzi had made the decision to stay at the house and watch the airing from there. Roshelle had agreed. "No need for you to follow me across town," she'd said. "Take a break."

As she drove out of the Valley and back across L.A. in the late night hours, she continued to wonder how Freddie could have known about the bracelet. Not even Newt was aware of the gift.

Mitzi was at the door to meet her when she came in. "Are you all right?" Her friend was nearly as upset as she was.

"I think so." Roshelle threw her wrap across the chair and collapsed onto the soft couch. "Can you believe that guy? Creating a story and then using it to bait those people in the audience."

"Well, fasten your seat belt, Rosh. That was mild compared to this."

Roshelle straightened. "What are you talking about?"

Mitzi reached into the nearby magazine rack and pulled out the latest tabloid and held it up for her to see.

Roshelle's hand flew to her mouth. "Oh, no! Mitzi, no."

The headlines screamed, LAUREL'S NEWEST RECORDING STAR FINDS THE LOVE OF HER LIFE. Beneath the headlines were photos—several photos. One was of her and Louis eating on the terrace at the Beverly Hills restaurant the night he gave her the bracelet. Several were of the two of them running and laughing on the beach. But the worst photo of all was the one of the two of them lying entwined on the towels at the moment he kissed her. The caption beneath read: "Lovely new recording artist, Roshelle Ramone, romping at Laguna with internationally known Louis Sarviano."

fifteen

The cold truth slowly seeped into her brain. In a matter of days, this tabloid would be on the shelves of every grocery store in every city in the nation. And where there was one, there would be ten more with the same story. Like wildfire in an Oklahoma hayfield in August, there was no way to stop it.

She felt sick and saddened. This wasn't how she planned to be known throughout the country. Suddenly, she realized how inexperienced and vulnerable she really was. She'd been told this was a crazy business but she hadn't counted on its being this crazy.

Slowly, she stood to her feet. "I think I know who's at the bottom of this," she said. "I have a phone call to make."

She closed herself in her studio and dialed Louis's number. "Do they pay you for divulging the information or do you just stage these little acts purely for pleasure?" she demanded as soon as she heard his voice on the line.

"Roshelle? You sound unhappy. Tell Louis what's the matter?"

"How could you do this to me? You staged this whole act and then called the photographers to stand by to get every shot they needed. Now it's not only aired on prime-time, live TV, but in every trashy tabloid from here to Long Island."

"Now, now," he cooed. "It wasn't quite that cut and dried. Nothing I ever said to you was a lie. I care for you a great deal."

"You expect me to believe that after all this?"

"Sweetheart, calm down. Don't you realize this is the best thing that could have happened to you? I know at least a dozen other greenhorns in this business who would give a right arm for this kind of publicity. I thought you'd be thrilled."

"You thought wrong," she snapped back.

"Roshelle, having your name out there just isn't enough these days. You have to create a gimmick, something to rouse interest. Even if you and I never saw one another again, this gives your public something to think about. . . something concrete to connect with your name.

"Excuse my modesty," he went on, "but being connected to the name of Sarviano will take you to the heights quicker than twenty successful albums combined. And I *do* care about you, that's why when the public relations people suggested to me—"

"You have the audacity to tell me they asked you to do this?"

"They merely asked my opinion about the best way to market you."

"Market me?" She felt like screaming. "Market me? I'm not a pound of sausage."

"In this business, you are closer to that than you might want to think, my dear." He paused a moment. "When they asked me, I felt you would be safer with me than anyone. And I truly did it because I care about you. I wanted to help you get off the ground quickly."

"But the album and the tour. . .it was all doing great. My music is all I need."

"Of course it is." His tone was patronizing. "Your music will take you a long way *after* the public knows who you are. Now they do."

Roshelle was at a loss. He had shot the release valve right off her head of steam. Nothing made any sense. Did it matter what people thought about whom she was with? He was right about everyone knowing her name through this. But what about the picture of them kissing? It was all terribly confusing.

"Let me take you to dinner tomorrow, darling. We'll talk and I'll try to explain to you how this business really works. Obviously, no one else has cared enough to do that."

"I'm not sure, Louis. I'll call you tomorrow and let you know."

A call in the wee hours of the morning roused her from a drugged sleeping pill-induced sleep. She could hardly get her bearings. She struggled to remember what city she was in and wondered why Mitzi wasn't taking the calls. But, as she pulled the receiver down to where she lay on the pillow, she realized she was home. Then she realized if she'd let it go, the answering machine would have caught it.

Suddenly, the sound of Benny Lee Camp's voice on the other end snapped her into reality. "Benny, where are you? I'm so glad to hear from you." His deep voice was like music to her ears and she was close to tears. Then she listened a little closer.

"You got ice water in your veins or what?" His voice slurred from the effects of too many drinks. "I tole the boys over and over that you'd call as soon as you could. But you never did. You never did. You think I care about being on your stage and riding on your name? Is that why you left me in the lurch? That why you didn't call me?"

"Oh, Benny. It isn't that at all." She grabbed pillows and

stuffed them behind her back so she could sit up. She willed her mind to clear.

"What d'ja think? That I'm some kinda mooch? I'm no mooch, Rosh. I just wanted to help you. Tha's all."

"Benny, you're drunk. Stop talking like a drunk. Talk sense."

"I tole the boys that other dolls might go to Hollywood and go off the deep end, but not our Roshelle. Not our Angel." She heard his voice catch. He was crying. "No, siree. Not our little Angel. But I was wrong. Dead wrong."

"Benny, stop it! This is crazy." She was sobbing. "I never meant to hurt you."

"I never minded so much when the tour started and you didn't want us. But, when I saw Fremont's show tonight. . . . You gonna marry that slimy weasel, Sarviano, Rosh? Huh? I thought you wasn't gonna marry anyone. You said you wasn't."

"I'm not, Benny. I'm not. I'm not going to marry anyone. Don't believe all that garbage. It's all for the press. . .for the publicity. You should know that. Benny, please listen to me."

She could hear him crying like a little baby, then the line went dead.

She didn't know from where he was calling. She could call Newt and find out. But then, she'd still be talking to a drunk man. She had to wait until he sobered up and then try to talk to him. Now, more than ever, she wished she'd called him first. . .just to talk. No matter what she told him about getting a new band, he would have accepted it, but this. . . .

"Roshelle." Mitzi was tapping at the door. "You talking in your sleep again?"

"I guess I was."

She pushed her head into the bedroom. "Pretty articulate for a dream. Sounded more like you were talking to someone on the phone after it rang."

"Oh, Mitzi," she groaned. "That was Benny."

"Don't tell me he saw the show?"

Roshelle was crying again, and she hated herself for it. All she could do was nod as she blew her nose on the tissue Mitzi handed her.

"The guy loves you, Roshelle. He's always loved you."

"He was drunk," she said as she gave a little gasp.

"That's understandable. After what he saw. Plus the tabloid stories. He's probably seen them, too."

"What am I going to do?" She punched at the pillow in her lap. "I've made a mess of everything."

"No you haven't, Rosh. You haven't made a mess of everything. First of all, you can't talk sense to a drunken man who's trying to drown his sorrow because his love's been spurned."

"I didn't spurn his love," she said through the sniffles.

"Okay. Let's just say you never encouraged it. That's hard on a man's ego. But his ego is not your concern now. Nor can you help what Louis did—or Freddie, either, for that matter. Right now, you can go back to sleep and rest. Next week you begin cutting the second album and that's where your heart really is...in your music. Just try to keep focused and stop letting all these people drive you to distraction."

"You're right, Mitzi. You're absolutely right. I can't let every little thing knock me down." She gave Mitzi a little hug. "I don't know what I'd do without you."

"Come on now, Rosh. You'd do just fine. You have more spit and vinegar than you give yourself credit for."

Roshelle wanted to believe that, but she couldn't. She

didn't have much resolve left at all.

The rest of the night was virtually sleepless. She paced the length of her bedroom. When she and Mitzi first designed the room in soft tones of mint green and peach, she thought it was lovely. But tonight it wasn't lovely at all. The sheer beauty of it was mocking her.

She seemed to be doing everything wrong. How could she be making so many crazy mistakes? It didn't matter that she wasn't in love with Benny Lee. She loved the person that he was and she hated herself for having hurt him.

And the truth was, she didn't really know how much longer she would be singing anyway. With each passing day, the pain in her throat increased and someday there'd be no more running from the truth.

The next morning she called Newt to ask the hotel where Benny was staying. "Sorry, sweets, they done checked out. They're on the road today." But he gave her the name and number of the hotel at their next stop.

She thanked him and then said, "Newt, is it too late to change my mind on doing a hymn on the next album? Like Ted wanted," she added in case he needed to be reminded.

"It ain't too late. Just like a woman. But it ain't too late. I'll call him and tell him right now. You know the title yet?"

"I'm. . .I'm not sure."

"He'll probably want to know. They're already doing layouts for the cover. I hate to press you, but. . . ."

And she hated being pressed. "Oh, all right. Tell him the name is 'In the Garden.' "

Newt gave a little chuckle. " 'In the Garden?' Funny name. You sure that's a religious song?"

"Trust me, Newt."

That's that, she thought as she hung up the phone. Vic had said hymns would help hurting people. Maybe in some way she could make up for having hurt Benny. . . maybe.

The first day of the recording session was agony. A singer could do a lot of glossing on stage to cover up for a few faults but the recording studio was like a refining fire. Late in the afternoon, her voice cracked and began to give out. She saw the pained look on the face of her soundman.

"Want to take a little break, Miss Ramone?" she heard him ask through her headset.

She shook her head. She'd push until she got it right. During breaks she downed pain pills and went right back in to work.

She requested that the hymn be left until last. The recording was already several days past schedule because so many songs had to be redone and Mr. Laurel was none too pleased.

"But he's a patient man," Newt told her on the side. "Don't let his gruffness fool you. He wants you to shine." But even Newt looked a little worried.

Finally, it was time to tackle the hymn. It had to be done and she dreaded it. She had no idea of what she was afraid.

For hours they worked. "Sorry, Miss Ramone," said the technician, "but it has no life. I know it's supposed to be a hymn, and hymns are more reserved, but you still need to put your whole self into it."

Why had she ever agreed to this fiasco? They were dead words to her. A sultry love song she could belt out, but this. . .?

Mr. Laurel was called in and Newt as well. They sat

down together to talk it over.

"I wanted you to do a religious song," Ted Laurel told her, "but I don't want you to bomb the album."

"Remember what that religious guy said?" Newt put in. "The one who has the studio in Tulsa? He said you made people cry. How'd you do that?"

Roshelle thought back. "For one thing I played my own accompaniment."

"You did what?" Ted asked.

"I played the piano myself as I sang."

"Well, why didn't you say so? We'll get a piano and move you into a bigger studio. That's simple. And what's this about some dude in religious recording? What's his name?"

"Victor Moran," Newt supplied the information.

"Call him. He knows more about this stuff than we do. Maybe he'll help us on this."

Roshelle panicked. "No, please—"

Newt touched her arm and gave her a look that said, "Don't ruffle any more feathers!"

She clenched her teeth and sat back quietly as Newt called his secretary to get Vic's number. In a matter of minutes, Mr. Laurel was talking to him on a conference call.

"I know this is a rather odd request, Moran. But I need a little favor," Mr. Laurel said in his usual blustery manner. "I'm willing to pay whatever it takes. Can you fly out here and help us with this religious number that Ms. Ramone wants to do?"

Roshelle didn't even need to listen. She knew what Vic's answer would be. He was on the next plane out.

sixteen

Victor Moran had a perfect opportunity to say "What changed your mind?" or "Glad you finally came around." But he said nothing and just set to work.

He checked out everything. First, he had private conferences with the soundmen and technicians then, he went over every note of the arrangement. They moved production to the larger studio with a grand piano. Finally, everything was ready.

"Only one more thing," he said to her. "Let me pray for you before we begin."

She froze. If there were snickerings among the crew, she never heard it. He unobtrusively sat down beside her on the piano bench and took her hands. It was probably the simplest prayer she'd ever heard. He asked for the power of the anointing of the Holy Spirit to be on her. And he asked it in Jesus' name. Then he smiled at her and walked out.

The soundman held up his hand and she watched as he brought it down. Suddenly, her fingers were moving easily over the keys and there was no pain in her throat. Her clear strong contralto voice never broke.

"He speaks, and the sound of His voice
Is so sweet the birds hush their singing;
And the melody that He gave to me
Within my heart is ringing.

And He walks with me, and He talks with me,
And He tells me I am His own,
And the joy we share as we tarry there,
None other has ever known."

Easily she breezed through all the verses, and twice again on the chorus. She barely remembered the recording and she didn't ask if it was a take. She knew it was. And she knew the prayer had everything to do with it. There were wet eyes in the sound room.

Blustery Mr. Laurel was saying, "Nice little song, Roshelle. Real nice song," as he gave her a condescending pat on the shoulder.

Newt, who was never without something to say, said nothing.

She thanked Vic.

"My pleasure," he answered simply, as his hazel eyes studied her. "You were great."

She heaved a sigh. It was over. Maybe now she could have some peace.

Roshelle tried repeatedly to contact Benny, but he refused her calls. Feeling that there was nothing else she could do, she finally gave up. What was the use?

Now all the tabloids announced that she had been jilted by her lover, the famous Sarviano. She had refused to see him again—other than for fitting sessions, that is. And, even then, he tried to tell her how much better her career would be if she linked up with him. He was probably right but, to Roshelle, it just wasn't worth it. One day she carefully wrapped the diamond bracelet and dropped it off at his studio.

The holidays came and went unceremoniously. In fact, Mitzi decided, of all things, to spend Christmas with her parents, so Roshelle was alone.

Album number two, turned out to be even more successful than the first and, several times, Newt tried to talk her into doing an album with the Moran Recording Studio.

"You're really good at that stuff," he said. "You even put a few goose bumps on this tough old hide of mine. Why, I always did think," he added, jabbing the air with his cigar, "that everybody oughta have a little bit of religion."

She ignored him. A little bit of religion. . .was that what she was doing? Funny. That was what she'd always accused Uncle Jess of having—a little bit of religion.

"I'm going out," Mitzi announced to her one rainy evening in late February.

"Out?"

Mitzi was dressed in a flowered jumpsuit with a perky ribbon in her hair. She looked like a teenager flushed with excitement. "Uh-huh. Out." She was grinning.

"Like on a date?"

"Like on a date!"

Roshelle was shocked. Mitzi never went anywhere unless it was running errands for Roshelle. Where could she have met anyone? "Do I know him?"

"As a matter of fact, you do."

Now her curiosity was thoroughly piqued. "Who?"

"Wait a few minutes and you'll see."

When the doorbell rang, Mitzi laughed and said, "You can answer it if you want."

Roshelle opened her front door to see a gangling, grinning six-foot Keel Stratton standing there, shaking off the rain. She couldn't believe it. "Why you goofy kid." She reached up as he leaned down so she could give him a hug. "What in heaven's name are you doing here?"

"I came to see Mitzi."

"No, I mean in California. Are you...is the band booked out here?" she asked hopefully, as she closed the door. Maybe now she could finally talk to Benny.

Keel shook his head. "I quit the band, Rosh. It sort of fell apart."

"Oh, no." She started to ask about it, but then she watched as his face lit up when Mitzi walked into the entryway.

"You two going to stand out there and talk all night?" Mitzi asked.

"Mitzi!" Keel stepped past Roshelle and grabbed Mitzi and swept her up in his arms. Then he kissed her soundly.

Slowly, Roshelle was beginning to understand that this had obviously been going on for quite some time.

As they sat down to talk, Mitzi served coffee and nut bread. They explained to Roshelle that they'd kept in touch by phone and letter ever since Roshelle's first stand in Reno.

"I was always crazy about her," Keel said, with his arm around Mitzi's shoulder, "but it just wasn't the right time. Now, with Benny drinking more and more, it's just not worth it to hang around the band. Plus, I'm tired of traveling." He looked deep into Mitzi's smiling black eyes. "I just want to settle down."

"How long have you been out here?" Roshelle asked, wondering if Mitzi had been sneaking around about this.

"Just a few days this time. But I've been out here a couple of other times before to see Mitzi."

"We didn't want to upset you," Mitzi put in. "He also came to my folks' place for Christmas." She grinned. "And they love him almost as much as I do."

"So, what are your plans?" Roshelle asked, as though it weren't obvious.

"We're going to get married right away," Keel said. "I've waited for her long enough."

They were waiting because of me, Roshelle realized.

"First thing for you to know, Rosh, is that I'll continue to work for you. I'll come here to work in the office every day just like always. Nothing is changed in that respect."

Nothing is changed? More like nothing will ever be the same. She had leaned on Benny and then he was gone. Next, she leaned on Mitzi and now she was gone. How crazy could she be? Nothing was certain except that she had only herself.

"Think about it, Rosh, old girl," she chided herself after the happy couple had left for the evening, "even if old Newt dropped dead tomorrow, you would still have to go on." Go on. That was it. That was her life. Corny as it might sound, the show must go on.

The wedding was a small affair. When Roshelle met Mitzi's parents, she wondered why the girl ever ran away. Mr. and Mrs. Wilson were a lighthearted pair, full of good humor. Looking back, Roshelle wondered if it had been more a case of "leaving home" rather than what Mitzi had called "running away."

Mr. and Mrs. Keel Stratton found an apartment in nearby Garden Grove. Keel snagged a job in a music store and did an occasional weekend gig. He even signed up for a few college classes. Roshelle had never seen Mitzi happier and she knew they would get along fine.

"She'll make a great wife," Roshelle told Keel following the wedding. "She cooks like a dream."

To which Keel replied, "I wouldn't care if she couldn't boil water."

The house was an empty shell without Mitzi there. Mitzi insisted, in agreement with Newt, that they run ads to find her a new "secretary," as they called it. But what they meant was a live-in companion. That made Roshelle feel like a candidate for the nursing home. In all honesty, she wanted someone there with her, but she didn't want anyone to know. At times the cavern of loneliness was so vast and so deep that she felt she'd been falling forever.

Newt, in the meantime, was planning another tour. There was no way she could ask Mitzi to go. By tour time, Newt insisted they find someone to at least be with Roshelle backstage on tour. She acquiesced. It turned out to be Blanche, an older sister of one of the backup singers. She was single, in her forties, and free to travel. When Roshelle interviewed her, she found her to be kind and compassionate.

The weekend before the tour began, Keel and Mitzi invited Roshelle to their house for Sunday dinner. Roshelle brightened at the thought of enjoying Mitzi's cooking once again.

"But on one condition," Mitzi said in a teasing tone.

"Conditions for a dinner invitation. Now I've heard everything," she shot back. "You've been in this business too long. Okay. What is it?"

"We've found a neat little church and we want you to go to Sunday service with us."

"Oh, Mitzi, give me a break." That was all she needed. Now these two.

"Every church isn't your Uncle Jess's church, you know," Mitzi said. "Why not come and visit, just for me?"

Roshelle thought of all the selfless giving Mitzi had poured out in those weeks and months that they were together and there was no way she could refuse.

The church was a sprawling building of the traditional southern California Spanish style. Greeters at the door were congenial as they handed out bulletins and shook hands, making everyone feel welcome. People in the foyer were chatting and children were running everywhere.

"It seemed to us like a family church," Mitzi was saying, noting all of the couples with small children. She gave Roshelle a little jab in the side. "Did I tell you Keel wants four kids, just like I do?"

"Good thing you agree on the small stuff," she quipped as she glanced inside the sanctuary. She was dreading this.

As they were seated in the soft padded pews, Roshelle glanced through all the announcements to have something to do. She stopped as she saw the title of the sermon: "The Myth of Hypocrisy."

She knew every selected hymn by heart—and all their verses. She supposed it was like riding a bike in that it just comes back to you. How she had always loved those old hymns.

Never once during the sermon did the pastor yell or beat on the pulpit. Rather, he spoke gently and kindly. The sanctuary itself was filled with the sound of the soft rustling of Bible pages turning as everyone had a Bible and was following the Scriptures he selected.

"Through the years," he said, "we've come to think of the word hypocrisy in only one vein. We've thought of it as people who act one way in church and another way out of church. We've almost taken delight as we gleefully point fingers at other people.

"The word *hypocrite* is a Greek word," he explained. "In the Greek theater it was their name for the actors. In order for the audience to see them, the actors wore large exaggerated masks. Therefore, a hypocrite was the person who played a part and wore a mask."

Like a stage face, Roshelle thought to herself.

"Basically the word simply means a person who pretends to be something he or she is not. Whether it has to do with church or not." As he spoke, the young pastor strode about the podium, directing his remarks to all parts of the church and at times turning around to speak to choir members who were seated behind him.

"We all wear masks," he went on. "Some of us wear heavier masks than others, depending on the measure of hurt we've experienced. Masks seemingly hide our pain. But living behind a mask can be lonely, frightfully lonely. Most of us are less than honest with our spouses, our loved ones, and our closest friends."

Mitzi reached over and squeezed Roshelle's hand.

"The good news is that the saving power of Jesus can cut through the heavy, exaggerated masks that we wear and that through an honest relationship with the Father-God, we can drop all the pretense and stop the hypocrisy."

Roshelle crossed and uncrossed her legs as she tried to get comfortable. For her, the service couldn't be over soon enough. She'd never before thought that perhaps she herself was a hypocrite. Hadn't she always said how she hated hypocrites? And yet she now realized that she wore the biggest mask of all—hiding her real feelings, hiding her fears, hiding her illness. She wanted out of that church fast.

Politely, she ate with Keel and Mitzi but, soon after dinner was over, she excused herself. "I still have a million things to do before the tour," she said.

"I'll be over tomorrow to help you pack," Mitzi said as she waved goodbye at the door.

Blanche was a fairly good companion backstage and was ready to take care of all the details. But she didn't know the ropes like Mitzi and she wasn't fun and silly and painfully honest like Mitzi. The farther along the tour went, the more Roshelle missed her dear friend. The loneliness was almost unbearable. Most nights she cried herself to sleep; the pain in her throat intensified as well.

It was halfway though the tour when it happened, in a theater in Philadelphia. She had made it through only the third number when she collapsed in a heap in front of hundreds of her fans.

True to her word, she sang until she dropped. The only trouble was, as she realized later, she'd never planned what to do after she dropped.

seventeen

Total rest, she was told—a frightening thought. Suffering from exhaustion, the papers reported. The rest of the tour was canceled and Roshelle was sent home. Newt was concerned; Mr. Ted Laurel was furious.

"Why didn't you take better care of yourself?" he bellowed. "You young stars are all alike. Think you don't need to eat or sleep."

Mitzi wanted to come and be with her, but she was now pregnant and suffering with the worst case of "all day" morning sickness. Roshelle could hear the torment in her friend's voice. "You need me, but I can't be there, Rosh. I'm so sorry. Every time I walk more than two steps at a time, I throw up."

Roshelle kept insisting that it was all right. In fact she felt worse for Mitzi than she did for herself.

The hours were unending. Blanche came in and out like a mother hen, fussing over her and bringing her all kinds of great things to eat.

But the nights were the longest. She listened to music; she played the piano; she read books; she paced the house—nothing helped. The agony was too much; the loneliness was too much.

"Uncle Jess always told me I'd be punished by God," she said to the silence. "Well, God, if You take away my voice, I guess that's about the worst kind of punishment I could ever imagine. Without my voice, I'm nothing.

Nothing."

From the bathroom cabinet she took down the bottle of sleeping pills—her friends, the sleeping pills. Why wait? Why continue suffering? It was too late for anything now.

She took the bottle downstairs to her studio. Probably she should write a note to Mitzi first, thanking her. . .and something to Janey. But then there was Benny. If only she could apologize to him. . .tell him how very sorry she was. Tears were streaming down her eyes as she thought of him.

And Vic. She sat down at the piano letting her fingers trail lightly over the keys picking out runs and chords. Vic had always been such a gentleman. . .so kind. . .so peaceful. Somehow she needed to apologize to him. . .and to thank him.

Strains of "In the Garden" spilled forth into the room. Total rest, the doctor had ordered her, but she couldn't stop the singing.

"And He walks with me and He talks with me. . . ."

She desperately needed someone with whom she could talk and walk. Someone who would be there always. Everything in her life was plastic and phony. . .and empty.

"Do You do that God?" she asked as her fingers continued the soft melody. "Are these words true? Do You walk and talk with people? Can that be real? That would be so wonderful. So wonderful to never be alone."

Suddenly, she was sobbing—sobs that were wrenching her insides. "Help me, God, please, help me. Please tell me I'm Your own, like the song says. I'm so lonely and so scared. I can't go another minute without knowing if You're there."

The sobs continued to shake her body until she was entirely spent. . .exhausted. The arrangement of the song was still on the piano and these words leaped at her from the page: "The melody that He gave to me. . . ."

She stared at the sheet. "Oh, God. That's it. You gave me the melody. *You* gave me the melody. You don't give and then take away." In a rush she ran up the stairs—just like Mitzi—two at a time. "You are with me. You are. I know. I can feel it!" She wanted to dance and jump and sing all at once.

There, in the bureau drawer beneath all the clothes, there it was—the Bible. What did that verse say? The one Vic was always giving to her? She knew right where to turn...where the violets were...where they had stained the page.

" 'I will praise the name of God with a song,' " she read aloud. "I will. It says 'I *will*.'" Suddenly, she was scouring Psalms for other verses that talked about singing. There were scores of them. Psalm 59:16 said "Yea, I will sing aloud of thy mercy in the morning. . . ."

She sprawled across the bed with the Bible in front of her, reading verse after verse, weeping as she read. "I will, Lord. You give me a chance, and I promise I will sing of Your mercy in the morning—every morning. Very loud!"

The next morning, after sleeping with no pills, she called Mitzi. "I'm going to Tulsa," she said. "There are a few things I need to take care of."

Quietly, Mitzi answered, "I thought there might be."

Next, she called Vic to let him know she was coming. "I'll need your help to get through this," she said meekly.

"I'm here for you. I'll meet you at the airport."

The moment Vic caught sight of her, he ran to her and wrapped her in his arms. "I've been so concerned ever since I heard—"

She put her fingers over his lips and then stood on tiptoe
to kiss him. Surprise registered in the hazel eyes but only
briefly. In a flash, he was kissing her fully with all the
passion of a man who had patiently waited for his love and
now the waiting was over.

Once in the car she explained the real cause for her
collapse. "Not just exhaustion as the paper said."

"I knew there was more," he said.

"I must talk to Dr. Beasley, to let him know I'm back and
to schedule the surgery. But first I have things to do in
Sandott."

"Alone?"

She reached for his hand. "Would you go with me?"

He kissed her hand. "I never want to leave your side."

She smiled at him. "One thing at a time."

The Oklahoma countryside was lush and green. The lacy
pink-and-white blossoms on the dogwood trees seemed to
float in space. Redwood trees spread their branches
everywhere. The beauty of God's creation was overwhelming, as though she'd never seen it before.

The little white church was much the same. When Vic
drove into the small graveled parking lot, she sat there
staring at it. "I grew to hate it so," she said softly, "and
them."

"Them, who?"

"Mother and Uncle Jess."

She stepped out of the car as he opened the door for her.
"Down in the basement," she said. He took her arm to
steady her.

The side door was unlocked and, being a weekday

afternoon, the place was deserted. He walked with her down the stairs. Everything was smaller than she remembered.

"I came inside that day because it was so hot outside. Down the steps here. There were old toys down here even though the place wasn't used much. I liked to play here, but Mother always told me not to. We lived a few doors down the street."

Vic switched on a light. The basement was much different now. . .light and airy. Concrete walls were painted in soft pastels; colorful partitions divided the room into classrooms.

"Tell me what happened," he said as they descended the last step.

"I was over here. . .behind stacks of folding chairs, hiding. I heard someone coming. I was scared. But it was only Uncle Jess. So I started to jump out and say "Boo." But then another person came down. It was Mother. They whispered and hugged and kissed in the dark. It was so awful. I felt like I was going to be sick, but I couldn't move." The tears began to flow.

Vic helped her to a small chair and made her sit down. "Then what happened?"

"It seemed so long. . .a long, long time." She gave a sigh. "Finally, they left."

"Is that all?"

She shook her head. "No." There was no way to stop the flood of tears or the deep sobs. "That night, I told Daddy. I told. I was so sorry I told. I didn't mean to tell. But I did."

"What did he do?"

"Nothing, then. He was so sweet and so good. He didn't

say anything. He just held me close. But the next day he
died. He died, Vic. . .and I killed him. They said it was
a heart attack, but I never believed that. I told him the
awful truth and it killed him!"

Vic put his arms around her and let her cry. "You were
just a little girl, Roshelle. A little girl. You didn't do
anything wrong. Do you hear me? You didn't do anything
wrong."

"I hated Mother and I hated Uncle Jess. But it was me.
I blamed them, but I did it. I killed him. Oh, I've wished
a million times that I'd never told him. Why couldn't I
have kept the awful secret?"

"Darling, listen to me." He took her shoulders and
pulled her back to look at her, wiping the tears from her
cheeks. "Your loving heavenly Father would never hold
you accountable for that action. You were only a child.
You've been focused on the wrong thing all these years
and it's destroying you. That guilt is too much for you to
bear."

"Help me, Vic. I want to be free. I want to forgive."

"The only thing you're accountable for is accepting
Jesus."

"But I've done that. . .when I was only eight." She
pointed upward. "Upstairs, there, at the altar."

"Well then, it's time to clear this up, once and for all.
Come here." He took her hand and led her to a little altar.
A bright red cloth covered it, an open Bible and a vase of
wilted flowers adorned it.

Together, they knelt down; together, they prayed. Later, when Vic helped her to her feet, the awful weight was
gone—completely gone. The relief was ecstasy. *Dear
God, maybe singing wasn't the only thing there was to life*

...to living. Maybe there was more, so much more—such as people, wonderful people.

He held her close. "Roshelle, I knew you were so tormented. I wanted to help, but I didn't know how."

"You've helped more than you'll ever know. Someday, I'll tell you all about it. Now, let's go pay a visit."

As the walked from the church, Vic stopped and pointed. "Look, Roshelle." The sidewalk from the church to the parking lot was lined with tiny clumps of lavender violets. He released her hand to reach down and pick a single flower. He pressed it into her hand and then kissed her. She smiled up at him through her tears.

"When I was unable to speak of my love to you," he said, "I prayed the flowers would speak for me."

"I've been an old fool," Uncle Jess told them as they sat with him in his small living room. The walker that he still used on occasions was nearby. "Your mother always loved me, Rachel, ever since she was in grade school. But I was older and thought of her as only a little kid. She was broken-hearted when I married. I thought she'd never get over it." He gave a shrug. "And I guess she never did."

Roshelle watched this old man in amazement. How could this be the man she'd been afraid of for all those years? "So she married Daddy instead?" she asked.

He nodded. "That she did. Out of anger and spite, she married your daddy. But then, when my Sally died, Cora wanted to divorce your daddy so we could get married. Me and Sally never had no kids, so I was all alone. But Cora was pregnant with you." He rubbed the gray stubble on his chin. "I couldn't never let her do that. Think how it would look. Well, she was more broken-hearted than ever."

Roshelle felt Vic squeezing on her hand. "Poor Mother," she heard herself saying. So this is what Janey meant about Cora's being wounded. But Roshelle never knew. No one ever told her.

"Roshelle thought she was responsible for her father's death because she told him she saw the two of you together," Vic explained to Uncle Jess. "Did your brother know about Cora's love for you?"

Uncle Jess gave a raspy little laugh. "Yep, I'm afraid he did. Everybody in four counties knew Cora loved me."

Vic gave Roshelle a knowing look. She sighed. All these years. The torture, the nightmares, the hate, the pain—now it was over.

"Then, when your daddy died, I was so guilt-ridden," Uncle Jess went on, "I felt I had to keep a tight rein on you." Grief lined the old man's face. "As I rode in that wailing ambulance to the hospital, I kept thinking, 'Lord, don't let me die. I can't face Jesus till I tell little Rachel how sorry I am.' Can you ever forgive me?"

"Last week, I might not have been able to, Uncle Jess, but today I can say 'Yes' and mean it. I do forgive you."

Tears coursed slowly down the leathery cheeks. She went over to him, sat down by him, and hugged him.

He reached around and patted her. "Your mother, bless her soul, in spite of all that's happened, she still loves me. I was so blind. Guilt and pride kept me from marrying her before. But, after coming so near to death's door, I've made up my mind, if she still wants this old coot, I'm going to marry her."

Roshelle looked back across the room at Vic and smiled. His eyes were wet as well. "Looks like we might be having two family weddings," he said softly.

eighteen

Her first awareness was that Vic was by her side. The fuzzy haze of anesthesia hung thickly in her mind.

Vic kept repeating, "Not malignant. The growths were not malignant, Roshelle." From a deep hollow well, she could faintly hear the words and the joy in his voice. "They got it all. You'll be fine. Just fine. You'll be singing your silken melodies in no time."

From the first intense pain that she experienced as she began to regain consciousness, it seemed impossible. But his words encouraged her daily. One of the first things she saw were the charming bouquets—at least a dozen—of violets all about the room. She gazed at them and marveled. Such love, such sweet love.

At first, she wasn't able to talk at all. After a few days she was able to manage a coarse whisper. That was the day Vic handed her the phone saying there was a special call for her. It was Benny Lee! She cried for sheer joy—and it hurt to cry.

"Don't cry, Angel," she heard his booming voice say. "Vic explained everything to me. You done it so I wouldn't know, you silly kid." She could hear the catch in his voice.

"I'm so sorry, Benny," she said in her loudest whisper. "I'm so sorry I hurt you. I never meant to—"

"If only you'd told me, I would have tried to help. You silly, sweet, beautiful kid. I'll always love you, Rosh. But

185

the Good Lord's provided just the right man for you."

She looked up at Vic and whispered, "Yes. The perfect one for me."

"That makes me happier than anything, Rosh. Just to know you're really happy." He took a breath. "Now listen, the boys and me are gonna get together and come out and see you soon. Real soon. Okay?"

"Okay, Benny. Thanks. . .for everything."

Vic took the phone and hung it up. Then he sat close to her on the edge of the bed.

"How long," she whispered, "before I can sing again? What does Dr. Beasley say?"

"I guess I didn't think to ask that question," he said. "I was more concerned with questions like, 'Is she all right?'" He kissed her forehead as he spoke the words. "Are you in a hurry?"

"God told me *He* gave me the melody. Now all I want to do is give them back to Him—singing songs to His glory."

He wrapped his arms around her and held her close. "I know the perfect recording studio who wants to offer you a lifetime contract."

Looking up into Vic's eyes and feeling the peace, strength, and love flowing from him into her own heart and being, she happily exclaimed, "I gladly accept that offer!"

A Letter To Our Readers

Dear Reader:

In order that we might better contribute to your reading enjoyment, we would appreciate your taking a few minutes to respond to the following questions. When completed, please return to the following:

Karen Carroll, Editor
Heartsong Presents
P.O. Box 719
Uhrichsville, Ohio 44683

1. Did you enjoy reading *Love's Silken Melody*?
   ☐ Very much. I would like to see more books
     by this author!
   ☐ Moderately
     I would have enjoyed it more if _____

   _____

2. Are you a member of *Heartsong Presents*? Yes   No
   If no, where did you purchase this book? _____

   _____

3. What influenced your decision to purchase
   this book? (Circle those that apply.)

Cover	Back cover copy
Title	Friends
Publicity	Other _____

4. On a scale from 1 (poor) to 10 (superior), please rate the following elements.

___Heroine   ___Plot

___Hero   ___Inspirational theme

___Setting   ___Secondary characters

5. What settings would you like to see covered in *Heartsong Presents* books?

_____

_____

6. What are some inspirational themes you would like to see treated in future books?_____

_____

_____

7. Would you be interested in reading other *Heartsong Presents* titles?   Yes   No

8. Please circle your age range:

| Under 18 | 18-24 | 25-34 |
| 35-45 | 46-55 | Over 55 |

9. How many hours per week do you read? _____

Name _____

Occupation _____

Address _____

City _____ State _____ Zip _____

···· Heartsong ····

ROMANCE IS CHEAPER BY THE DOZEN!

Any 12 *Heartsong Presents* titles for only $26.95 *

Buy any assortment of twelve *Heartsong Presents* titles and save 25% off of the already discounted price of $2.95 each!

plus $1.00 shipping and handling per order and sales tax where applicable.

HEARTSONG PRESENTS TITLES AVAILABLE NOW:

____HP 1 A TORCH FOR TRINITY, *Colleen L. Reece*
____HP 2 WILDFLOWER HARVEST, *Colleen L. Reece*
____HP 3 RESTORE THE JOY, *Sara Mitchell*
____HP 4 REFLECTIONS OF THE HEART, *Sally Laity*
____HP 5 THIS TREMBLING CUP, *Marlene Chase*
____HP 6 THE OTHER SIDE OF SILENCE, *Marlene Chase*
____HP 7 CANDLESHINE, *Colleen L. Reece*
____HP 8 DESERT ROSE, *Colleen L. Reece*
____HP 9 HEARTSTRINGS, *Irene B. Brand*
____HP10 SONG OF LAUGHTER, *Lauraine Snelling*
____HP11 RIVER OF FIRE, *Jacquelyn Cook*
____HP12 COTTONWOOD DREAMS, *Norene Morris*
____HP13 PASSAGE OF THE HEART, *Kjersti Hoff Baez*
____HP14 A MATTER OF CHOICE, *Susannah Hayden*
____HP15 WHISPERS ON THE WIND, *Maryn Langer*
____HP16 SILENCE IN THE SAGE, *Colleen L. Reece*
____HP17 LLAMA LADY, *VeraLee Wiggins*
____HP18 ESCORT HOMEWARD, *Eileen M. Berger*
____HP19 A PLACE TO BELONG, *Janelle Jamison*
____HP20 SHORES OF PROMISE, *Kate Blackwell*
____HP21 GENTLE PERSUASION, *Veda Boyd Jones*
____HP22 INDY GIRL, *Brenda Bancroft*
____HP23 GONE WEST, *Kathleen Karr*
____HP24 WHISPERS IN THE WILDERNESS, *Colleen L. Reece*
____HP25 REBAR, *Mary Carpenter Reid*
____HP26 MOUNTAIN HOUSE, *Mary Louise Colln*
____HP27 BEYOND THE SEARCHING RIVER, *Jacquelyn Cook*
____HP28 DAKOTA DAWN, *Lauraine Snelling*
____HP29 FROM THE HEART, *Sara Mitchell*
____HP30 A LOVE MEANT TO BE, *Brenda Bancroft*
____HP31 DREAM SPINNER, *Sally Laity*
____HP32 THE PROMISED LAND, *Kathleen Karr*
____HP33 SWEET SHELTER, *VeraLee Wiggins*
____HP34 UNDER A TEXAS SKY, *Veda Boyd Jones*
____HP35 WHEN COMES THE DAWN, *Brenda Bancroft*
____HP36 THE SURE PROMISE, *JoAnn A. Grote*
____HP37 DRUMS OF SHELOMOH, *Yvonne Lehman*
____HP38 A PLACE TO CALL HOME, *Eileen M. Berger*

(If ordering from this page, please remember to include it with the order form.)

· ·

HPS DECEMBER

··········Presents··········

LOVE A GREAT LOVE STORY?

Introducing Heartsong Presents —
Your Inspirational Book Club

Heartsong Presents Christian romance reader's service will provide you with four never before published romance titles every month! In fact, your books will be mailed to you at the same time advance copies are sent to book reviewers. You'll preview each of these new and unabridged books before they are released to the general public.

These books are filled with the kind of stories you have been longing for—stories of courtship, chivalry, honor, and virtue. Strong characters and riveting plot lines will make you want to read on and on. Romance is not dead, and each of these romantic tales will remind you that Christian faith is still the vital ingredient in an intimate relationship filled with true love and honest devotion.

Sign up today to receive your first set. Send no money now. We'll bill you only $9.97 post-paid with your shipment. Then every month you'll automatically receive the latest four "hot off the press" titles for the same low post-paid price of $9.97. That's a savings of 50% off the $4.95 cover price. When you consider the exaggerated shipping charges of other book clubs, your savings are even greater!

THERE IS NO RISK—you may cancel at any time without obligation. And if you aren't completely satisfied with any selection, return it for an immediate refund.

TO JOIN, just complete the coupon below, mail it today, and get ready for hours of wholesome entertainment.

Now you can curl up, relax, and enjoy some great reading full of the warmhearted spirit of romance.